IN SHEEP'S
CLOTHING

DAVID ARCHER

A
NOAH WOLF
THRILLER

IN SHEEP'S
CLOTHING

Get David Archer's Starter Library FOR FREE

Sign up for the no-spam newsletter and get THE WAY OF THE WOLF, plus the first two novels in David's bestselling *Sam Prichard* Series, and lots more exclusive content, all for free.

Details can be found at the end of IN SHEEP'S CLOTHING

"Beware the wolf in sheep's clothing."

ONE

Noah Wolf walked into the conference room with Sarah Child, his transportation officer and apparent girlfriend, beside him. Neil Blessing, his computer and intelligence specialist, was already there. Allison Peterson, the director of E & E, and Donald Jefferson, her Chief of Staff, shook hands with them and pointed to the coffee and doughnuts that were always present in these meetings. Moose Conway, who was Noah's backup muscle, arrived only a few moments later and the briefing got underway.

"You've had almost four months to take it easy since you all got yourselves torn up on the last mission, so we've got an easy one for you, this time," Jefferson said. "No international travel this time; you're going to be working right here at home. The DEA has identified high-ranking members of the Angelos Michoacan drug cartel operating from a base in the Midwest, and has requested our services to eliminate them. There are five primary targets in all, and it's necessary that they're eliminated in such a way that it sends a message back to the cartel."

"I've got a question," Neil said. "If they know who they are, why don't they just go and arrest them? Why send us in?"

"That's a valid question," Allison said, "so I'll give you a straight answer. DEA and FBI have been tracking them for a few months now, but these people are smart. They don't allow anything to happen that could provide evidence to back up a warrant or lead to an arrest. DEA has picked up dozens of their dealers and mules, but none of them are allowed to know enough to give us any valid intelligence. This is a case where the best way to put a stop to their enterprise is to simply cut off the head."

Neil was shaking his head. "Wait a minute, wait a minute, let me get this straight," he said. "They don't have enough evidence to arrest these guys, but they have enough to say let's just kill them and get it over with? Correct me if I'm wrong, but I thought we were still in America."

Allison smiled her famous dragon-lady smile at him. "We have detailed intelligence from before these people came to the United States, positively identifying them as major players in the cartel. The DEA can prove that many of the dealers and mules they've arrested have had regular contact with them, but nothing that adds up to sufficient evidence to get a warrant. Since those dealers are distributing some pretty high-grade heroin and cocaine with all the chemical signatures to prove it's coming from the Angelos cartel, I didn't have any problem authorizing the sanctions."

Neil shrugged but settled back into his chair without any further comments. Allison nodded to Jefferson, and he went on.

"As I said, the idea is to make a statement with their termination," he said. "We want the cartel to think long and hard before they send any more people or product into our country. How you go about it is entirely up to you, Camelot, but the messier you can make it, the better. The Angelos Cartel is one of the most brutal in the world, and the FBI credits this particular group with at least three-dozen murders here on our soil. Some of those murders were execution-style, and rumor has it that they were ordered because of a few dollars missing from the daily take. The worst of it is that when the Angelos decide to take you out, they don't just stop with you. They take out your entire family as well, eliminating, as they put it, 'you and your seed from the gene pool' completely."

"I want to say something before we finish up here," Allison said. "Noah, I want you to make it look like the evil they've been dishing out came back to haunt them. Each of the cartel members in Columbia has a family with them. I'd personally like to see you give them back exactly what they've been handing out."

Sarah gasped. "You want him to kill their families?"

Allison didn't even blink. "Yes," she said, looking Noah in the eye. "If it's feasible and can be done without significantly putting you or the team at risk, that's exactly what I want, and before you go all moral on me, Sarah, listen up. The higher-ranking members of any drug cartel tend to operate like a family business. As long as any member of the family is still around, business goes on as usual. Besides that, the cartels use terror tactics to try to keep people in line, which means that a lot of people who never intended to get involved in the drug trade are too frightened to try to get out. Feeding them the same slop they dish out might throw a bit of a worry into their leadership, but it's also almost certain to strengthen the spines of the people they run roughshod over. Maybe we can get those people to rise up against the cartels and help to shut them down for good."

She paused for a moment, as if thinking. "That being said, I should point something out. Alejandra Gomez, one of the members in Columbia, has a two-year-old daughter and a three-year-old son. No matter how I feel about their tactics, I can't sanction the murder of children, so leave them alone. Other than that, the next youngest is Eduardo Menendez's sixteen-year-old son, Manuel, but he's a soldier in his father's operation with a half-dozen kills to his credit already. The rest of the family members are brothers and sisters and aunts and uncles. They tend to take the whole clan with them when they go somewhere."

Jefferson had stopped talking and let her hold the floor, but then he nodded. "As terrible as it sounds, this really is the best way to handle the situation."

Noah never broke eye contact with Allison. "I'll do it," he said. "And I'm glad you clarified that about the kids. I'll make sure they're not around before I strike."

There was an uncomfortable silence for a few seconds, but then Jefferson cleared his throat and said, "I've got your ID kits ready, along with the dossier on your targets, so you can leave whenever you're ready. Columbia is a college town, so it has a ready-made drug market. We believe the cartel chose it as their central distribution point because of its location, and because transportation to just about anywhere else in the country is readily available there. There is an airport, but I'm going to suggest that you drive in, rather than fly."

"You'll want to swing by the Armory," Allison said, "and pick up any weapons you might want to take along, and I've already told Wally to expect you. You'll get your vehicles there, and I'm sure he's got some other toys that might come in useful on this mission."

Packets were passed to each of the men, and Sarah received a leather purse. Inside, they found wallets and the special, ultra-secure cell phones used during missions, and Noah also received a thick file folder that contained information on all of the targets. They all glanced at their IDs and scanned through the wallets and such to learn more about who they were supposed to be for this mission.

Noah would be Wyatt Wilson. His wallet contained a driver's license, several credit cards and a few hundred dollars in cash, along with several photos. Some of them showed Noah with an older couple, others had him posing with Sarah or another woman, and one showed him with a couple of young boys. There were also numerous worn-out business cards, a few scribbled notes and a long-compressed condom. The data sheet that came with the wallet explained that the people in the digitally constructed photos were his parents, an older sister, a girlfriend (Sarah) and two nephews.

Moose's new name was Jimmy McCormick, while Neil became Leonard Kincaid. That left only Sarah, who found that she was now known as Rosemary Wingo. Her data sheet told her that she was Wyatt Wilson's fiancé, and Sarah's eyes grew wide when she saw a modest but lovely engagement ring in a plastic bag attached to it.

She took it out and slipped it onto her finger, then glanced up at Allison and caught the woman grinning at her. Sarah blushed as she grinned back, but the men seemed not to notice.

Jefferson cleared his throat to get their attention. "Since this is your first time running a mission domestically, I want to point out one thing you need to know. On each of your driver's licenses is a magnetic strip. If you happen to be arrested for anything connected to the mission, tell them that you are a federal agent working undercover and insist that the officers run that strip through a reader. It will instruct them to contact the US State Department, and arrangements will be made immediately for your release."

Noah looked at Allison. "What kind of timetable do we have on this?"

"If it takes more than a week," Allison replied, "I might begin to wonder if you're slipping. It's not about getting it done quickly, though, it's about making sure there's no doubt that they were taken out deliberately and as a result of their activities. To the rest of the world, it can look like a drug war, but I want the cartel back in Mexico to know exactly what it is: Uncle Sam got pissed and had them whacked. Taking out their whole families, especially in an obviously orchestrated way, would be beyond the capability of any of our local drug gangs. They'll get the message."

"I'll play it by ear," Noah said. "What kind of techniques does the cartel use in executions?"

"The usual," Allison said. "Bullet to the head, decapitation, evisceration, bombings. It depends on just how strong a message they're trying to send. You'll need to think the way they do."

Noah nodded. "I can handle it," he said. He rose from his seat at the table and collected the rest of the team by eye. They shook hands all around and followed him out of the room. A moment later, three vehicles left the underground parking garage. Neil and Moose headed home, while Noah took Sarah along in his Corvette to begin choosing equipment.

Noah flashed his ID at the guard shack that marked the entrance to the restricted area of the gigantic compound. Taking up almost half of the fifteen-square-mile region, this was where the top-secret aspects of E & E could be found, and the local residents simply thought it was some sort of military complex. Noah drove along the twisting, mile-long roadway and emerged into a cluster of large concrete buildings.

He pulled up in front of the R & D building and was greeted at the entrance by one of their security officers. Once again he showed his ID, and Sarah produced her own. The guard studied them intently for several seconds, comparing the photographs to the faces in front of him before he handed them back and allowed them to pass into the main hallway.

Wally Lawson stepped out of one of the rooms off that hallway, saw Noah and broke into a big grin.

"Camelot!" Wally shouted, and then he reached out and grabbed Noah's hand, pumping it vigorously. "It's good to see you. Man, oh man, have I got some goodies to show you today!"

Noah's eyebrows rose slightly. "We got a mission," he said. "I was told to come to you for vehicles and to see what else you might have."

Wally's eyes went wide and his face lit up in a gigantic smile. "Oh, great! What kind of mission? Where at? You do know that I'm cleared for all that information, right?"

"Yes," Noah said, "I've been told that. It's a domestic mission, the elimination of some high-ranking cartel members and their families. They've set up an operation in Columbia, Missouri, and I gather their drugs are flooding the streets throughout the Midwest, maybe even a lot further."

Wally began chewing on his bottom lip, his eyes darting all around as he thought about what Noah had told him. "Okay,

okay," he mumbled. "Okay, I've got just the thing for you! Come on, you're gonna love this!"

Wally took off down the hall without even waiting to see if Noah and Sarah followed, and they fell in behind. He led them to one of the development rooms further down the hall and motioned for them to follow him inside.

Within the room were two technicians, a man and a woman. They looked up, curious, and Wally introduced them to Noah. "Jazz, Lenny," Wally said, addressing the woman first, "this is Camelot! Camelot, meet Jasmine and Lenny. These two are a pair of the brightest and most diabolical minds you'll ever find anywhere, and we were lucky to get them."

Noah shook hands with both of the technicians and introduced Sarah, as well. When all of the introductions and handshakes were over, Wally spoke up again. "Okay, kids, show 'em what you've got."

Jasmine smiled. "I'm guessing you're familiar with plastic explosives, right? Well, Lenny and I have come up with a whole new formula that is half again as powerful when it explodes, but a dozen times more stable. As a result, we're able to do things with it that no one has ever done before. Take a look over here."

She pointed to where Lenny was standing beside a workbench that held what appeared to be a very large suitcase. He opened the lid and raised it, and a metal framework expanded upward until it made a cube that measured about thirty inches on a side. There were a number of components inside the framework and a lot of circuitry on the outside.

Tucked inside the lid of the case was what appeared to be one large plastic tank and several smaller ones. The big one contained a thick, white liquid, while the others contained thinner liquids in various colors.

A slot near the bottom of the case opened up, and something slid out. A second later, it opened to become the keyboard and monitor of a computer.

"This is a high-speed 3-D printer," Lenny said, "but instead of using plastics, it uses our formula of plastic explosive. The explosive itself is a neutral color, sort of an off white, but this printer can inject color into each cubic millimeter of the plastic, so you can make an object that is intricately detailed. It can blend colors to give you exactly the shade you need, anything from dull plastic to shiny metallic. Let me show you what it can do."

Lenny turned toward the small computer that was attached to the case. He tapped the keys for a moment, calling up a file in a CAD program, and it displayed a three-dimensional image of an intricately painted figurine of a clown. He used a trackball to rotate the image on the screen, then pointed at some parts on the upright supports of the printer.

"Another difference between this printer and others is that this one is also a 3-D scanner. You simply set an object on the print bed and tell it to scan through the computer, and it does the rest. Those lasers will get an absolutely accurate measurement of the shape and size of the object you're scanning." He pointed at the screen in front of them again. "Now, I scanned this figurine in a couple of months ago, as we were first testing the printer. Notice how it has almost a dozen different colors, counting the clown's face and costume, right? Now, watch this." He tapped another key and the printer's nozzle began moving over the print bed at the bottom of the machine.

"That's going a lot faster than the ones I see on TV," Noah said.

Jasmine, who was standing beside him, smiled. "It's called a Rep Rap, which means Replicating Rapid Prototyper. That clown is about nine inches tall, and a normal 3-D printer would take up to four hours or more to complete it. This one can do it in about eight minutes."

Lenny grinned at them. "That's because of our formula," he said. "Most 3-D printers use a solid string of plastic, melting it a little at a time to put it where it belongs. Ours is liquid, and the hot print head actually causes it to solidify where we want it."

"Look," Sarah said, "I can see its feet already. How do you make them so shiny? That almost looks like real ceramic."

"Well, in a way, it is ceramic," Lenny said. "Along with the color, we add a glazing agent that crystallizes quickly. As it's pushed through the hot nozzle, the glazing agent melts and gives it that shiny-wet look. Without special analytical equipment, you'd never be able to tell it isn't a real ceramic figurine."

Suddenly, the print head rose away from the work it was doing, and a mechanical arm swung down from the top of the machine. A small cylindrical object, about an inch long and a quarter-inch in diameter, was placed inside one of the hollow legs that stood there. The arm then moved away, and the print head resumed its work, securing the little device in place.

"Before you ask, I'll just tell you what that was," Lenny said. "That was the detonator. It has a small charge of its own, a super small battery and a microcircuit receiver that can be activated manually, or set to go off at a certain time or after X number of minutes. Give it a few more moments, it's almost done, and then we can show you what it's capable of."

It took about four more minutes to complete the figurine, and then Lenny invited Noah to remove it from the printer. He picked it up and felt its weight, then ran his fingers over the surface.

"You're right," he said. "If I hadn't watched you print it out, I'd never know this wasn't real. I'm assuming it's pretty stable? What would happen if I dropped it right now?"

Jasmine grinned. "Not a thing," she said. "This stuff is so well bonded together that it wouldn't even break. Go ahead, try it if you want to."

Sarah's eyes went wide, and she shook her head at Noah. "That's okay," he said, "I'll take your word for it. What about impact, or fire? I know that C4 won't explode unless it's got a detonator, but it will burn."

Lenny took the figurine from his hand and set it on a workbench, then picked up a propane torch and aimed the flame at its head. After several seconds, it was obvious that the flame was having no effect, so he turned it off and picked up what looked like an eight ball from a pool table.

"I made this the other day," he said, "but I don't really need it." He set it on the workbench and then picked up a small, heavy hammer. He grinned at Sarah and then brought the hammer down as hard as he could onto the ball. It shattered into several pieces, and they saw that it had been hollow. Inside was one of the small detonators, stuck to the inner wall of one of the pieces.

"You could shoot holes through it, and it wouldn't explode. It takes a special detonator that uses Triaminotrinitrobenzene and Diaminodinitroethene in combination to produce enough heat and shock to set it off, but boy, when it does! Come on, we'll show you."

Lenny walked into what appeared to be a steel box with a window in it, and they could see through a square, obviously thick window as he placed the clown figurine onto a heavy iron block. He stepped back out into the room and closed the door of the box, which they could see looked a lot like the door on a major bank vault. Lenny spun the wheel on the outside of the door to secure it and then stepped over beside Noah and Sarah as they looked in the window. Jasmine and Wally stood right behind them.

Lenny reached over to pick up a small black box from the workbench and handed it to Noah, who looked it over. There was a small numerical keypad and a single-line display on the front, a red button that sat in a depression on the side, and an open round socket on the top. "That's the detonator remote," he said. "Just push the red button whenever you're ready, but keep your eyes on the clown."

Noah glanced at Sarah, who looked very nervous, then grinned at her. He turned his eyes back to the clown that he could see through the window and brought his thumb down on the button.

A muffled *boom* reverberated around the room, and Sarah grabbed onto Noah's arm to keep from falling as vibrations shook the solid concrete floor beneath her feet. Her eyes were wider than before and she looked at Noah as if in shock.

"Holy cow," she said.

Noah's own eyebrows were pretty high, as he leaned close to the window to try to see inside. When the clown had exploded, the window had been filled with flames that were bright red and yellow, but that had lasted only a couple of seconds. He could see no visible residue, other than the obvious burn marks on the walls and on the block.

"That's pretty impressive," he said. "And I can see a lot of uses for it." He pointed at the printer. "How much does it weigh?"

"About sixty pounds," Jasmine said, "but that's with all its tanks loaded. You can also carry extra material and inks. The compound is extremely stable, and can't explode without a detonator."

"Does it take a separate detonator and remote for each piece you make?"

Lenny pointed at the remote that was still in Noah's hand. "You need a separate detonator for each one, but that remote will handle them all. All you have to do is insert a detonator into the hole on top and you'll see the numbers zero through nine appear on the display. One through nine are the channels available and you simply press the number of the channel you want that particular detonator to respond to. That programs it, then you just put it into the grip on the detonator placement arm. The computer will decide the best place to put it inside whatever you make. Then, when you want to set it off, you just press the channel button and then the red button. Or, if you choose zero, it goes into timer mode. You'll see a 1 and a 2. If you choose 1, it will let you put in a time based on a twenty-four-hour clock, and then it will ask for a date. That sets the detonator to go off at a particular time on a particular day. If you choose 2, on the other hand, it asks you for the number of minutes you wanted to wait before detonating, and you can go up to 525,600 minutes. That's the number of minutes in a year. It's that easy."

"What frequency does it work on? What's the chance that a stray signal might set it off?"

"There's no chance, none at all. The signal is encrypted, a string of numbers so long that you couldn't fake it in a million years. You can have a thousand devices transmitting on the same frequency, and none of them could ever set these off."

"So, if I want to detonate manually, I can have up to nine devices ready to go and set them off in whatever order I want, right?" Noah asked.

Lenny nodded. "Yes, or you can have more than one device on a single channel. As long as you're in range of all of them, they all go off at once. The detonator has a range of about three-quarters of a mile."

Noah said. "How many of those clowns could it make on a single fill-up?"

"Probably about thirty," Jasmine said. "Making figurines and such, you just make it hollow. The outside is about a quarter-inch thick, but that gives you plenty of explosive power, as you saw. If that explosion had been set off in an average house, it probably would have taken out about half of it. Walls, ceiling, roof, you name it."

Noah looked at her for a moment, then asked, "So a smaller object that was solid, not hollow, would have just as much effect?"

"Or more. The compound tends to reverberate, actually build on its own shock wave. The denser the item you make, the more explosive pressure you get from its detonation. The clown was nine inches tall, but hollow. A three-inch clown that was solid, molded around a detonator, would deliver about half again as much power as the hollow one."

"Okay, one more question. How do I get the things I want to make into the computer?"

Lenny grinned. "There are two options. Number one, just use the built-in scanner if the object is small enough to fit inside. Number two, we've adapted the 3-Sweep software that can make a 3-D model from a single photograph, so you can just take a few pictures of something, extract them into 3-D, and then print it out. Or number three, if you know how to use CAD, you can literally just design something and then print it out. The software in the computer already has about fifteen thousand 3-D images stored in it."

Noah stood and looked at the printer for several seconds, then turned to Wally. "I want one, and give me a couple of refills on the explosives and inks. I'll need a few dozen of the detonators, too."

Wally grinned from ear to ear. "I had a feeling you might like that," he said. "Would it be safe to assume that your cartel people might be receiving some presents in the near future?"

"Yeah," Noah said. "They're likely to think I'm Santa Claus."

TWO

Wally led them through several other sections of this facility, but Noah didn't choose any other devices. He ended the tour by leading them out into a parking area behind the building. There were numerous vehicles there, ranging from beat-up old pickup trucks to new luxury cars. Two security guards sat in a small air-conditioned office, and they waved at Wally.

"We'll need two cars," Noah said. "Anything special about these?"

Wally grinned again. "Nothing like James Bond's cars," he said, "but don't let their looks deceive you." He pointed to a line of cars and pickup trucks. "Every vehicle in that line has a lot more power than you would expect. We're talking the eight hundred horsepower range, so don't let it get away from you."

"Eight hundred horsepower?" Sarah asked, incredulously. "That's pretty serious."

Noah looked at her, and one side of his mouth lifted in what she thought was almost a grin. "Pick the one you want," he said, and then pointed at a small utility van. "We'll take that one, besides whatever Sarah wants. How long would it take to get a florist's logo on the side?"

"About an hour," Wally said. "We've got about ten thousand logos already made up, it's just a matter of printing it out and sticking it on. No addresses, no phone numbers; people don't pay much attention to those, anyway. I'll get that started right now." He took a walkie-talkie out of one of his pockets and spoke into it for a minute. "Okay, I was wrong," he said as he looked at Noah again. "Our camouflage division has a flower shop sign ready to go. They'll be out to put it on in just a few minutes."

"Sounds good," Noah said. "What about license plates, registration, insurance cards?"

"We can put any state tag on it you want, and create registration and insurance cards to match. The van's registration, for instance, will come back to a flower company with its headquarters here. Incidentally, any of these vehicles are disposable. If you need to ditch one, just go ahead. The registrations trace back to a dummy outfit, a dead end. If you crash one or have to leave it behind for some reason, don't worry about it."

Sarah walked around the lot for a few moments, then pointed at a silver Chrysler 300 sedan. "My father always said that was one of the best-handling machines he'd ever driven," she said. "If I'm going to have that much horsepower, I want something that can cope with it."

"You're going to love that one," Wally said. "Incidentally, it's all-wheel drive, with some very special tires that grip the road like nothing you've ever seen. That sucker will take a corner at seventy miles an hour if you really want to, but that's just the beginning. Let me show you some of the special features of this car." He went to the guardhouse and got the keys to both of the vehicles they had chosen, tossed the van keys to Noah and then walked directly to the Chrysler. Sarah followed him and slid behind the wheel at his invitation.

"Okay, you're gonna love this. This car is one of several that we designed specifically to help you teams escape when things go bad, or duck the local police as necessary. In order to accomplish that, we've added some things you're sure to like." He pointed at a spot on the dashboard and told her to press it. A panel opened up and she saw a dozen buttons arranged in rows of four. "The top row of buttons changes the license plate. There are four different sets installed, and each one is registered to a car identical to this one. Pretty cool, right?"

Sarah was grinning at him. "That's slick," she said.

Wally held up a finger. "But you haven't seen the best part. The next two rows of buttons do something even more special. Push the second button, and you'll see."

Sarah looked at him suspiciously. "It's not gonna, like, throw me out of the car, is it?"

"No, no," Wally laughed. "Trust me, just push it."

Sarah eyed him for another couple of seconds, then reached over and pushed the button. She was watching the dashboard as if expecting something to happen there, when Wally said, "See what I mean?"

She looked up, and that's when she realized that the silver hood of the car had suddenly become a dark green. Her eyes went wide. "Did this car just change color?"

Noah was standing stock still, his head cocked to one side as he kept his eyes on the car. "It did," he said. "One second it was silver and the next it was green."

Wally laughed and did a little dance. "Isn't that awesome? It's called electroluminescence; it uses varying amperage of electrical current to cause prismatic crystals within the paint to slightly alter their shape and size, which results in reflecting a different color for the eye to see. Try another button, I never get tired of watching this stuff work."

Sarah pushed another button and the car suddenly became bright yellow. Another button turned it to a deep blue, and yet another made it red. "Okay, this is just absolutely incredible. How do I get a paint job like this on my car?"

"Oh, you can get it, but it won't be quite as good as this. We just happened to have the resources to take the technology to a whole new level. The stuff that's available commercially isn't quite as good as this, but it does work."

Two men came out a moment later and applied a genuine-looking florist's logo to the van. Noah and Sarah drove both of the vehicles around to the front of the building, where a man met them with a handcart carrying the printer and several other boxes. He loaded everything into the back of the van, and Noah followed Sarah back to his house. The Corvette would be safe in Wally's care until they returned.

The next stop was the Armory. Sarah followed Noah inside and waited while he selected a couple of assault rifles and a pair of Interdynamic MP9 machine pistols, then loaded several cases of ammunition with them into the van.

Moose's car was parked by Neil's trailer, which sat on Noah's land. Moose and Neil were sitting at a table on his deck, with an umbrella over them to block the sun's bright rays. They waved as Sarah and Noah pulled in, then got up and began walking over toward the bigger house.

"Hey, Boss," Moose called out as he pointed at the van. "We going into the flower business?"

"Yep," Noah said. "Neil, you know how to use CAD software?"

Neil sneered at him. "I knew how to use that when I was in kindergarten," he said. "Why?"

"Wait just a minute," Sarah said, "you guys have got to see this!" She spent the next five minutes showing off the Chrysler's special abilities, and both Moose and Neil were fascinated.

Finally, Noah called a halt to the show. He opened the back of the van and told Moose to grab the big suitcase, bring it inside and set it on the table, and a few moments later Neil's eyes grew wide as the 3-D printer rose from within the concealing suitcase. He did a double take when the computer slid out of the base.

"Holy crap," he said. "Is that what it looks like?"

"Yes and no," Noah said. "It's a 3-D printer, and very fast, but you don't want to be making toys with it." He pointed at the big tank. "It turns that liquid into solid objects which just happen to be extremely explosive. The stuff is very stable, and can't go off without a special detonator. See that little arm off to the side? That thing puts the detonator inside whatever you're making, and there's a way to program it so that we can make it go off when we want it to."

Noah and Sarah spent the next half hour explaining it all to Neil, while he played with the CAD and 3-Sweep programs on the computer and made himself familiar with them. To the surprise of no one, both he and Moose wanted to see the explosive in action, so Noah gave the okay. There were thousands of 3-D images already available in the software, so Neil chose a mouse figurine that was about three inches tall. It would print out the figurine, leaving it hollow.

Noah picked up one of the detonators and plugged it into the remote, then programmed it to channel 1. He set the detonator in the arm's grip, and then nodded at Neil.

The printer began working and the mouse was finished in about three minutes. Noah reached in and picked it up, flipping it casually in the air as he walked out his front door. Sarah followed right behind him, but Moose and Neil were watching closely as he tossed it from hand to hand.

"Hey, Boss, don't you want to be a little more careful with that?" Moose asked.

"Relax, Moose," Sarah said. "Like he told you, it's very stable. It won't go off until he tells it to."

Noah led the way out into the yard and walked directly to a dead tree. The tree was hollow, and he put the little mouse inside a hole near its roots. "I've been meaning to take this tree out, anyway," he said. "Let's see how well this stuff really works."

They backed off about a hundred feet and then Noah turned on the remote. He pressed 1, then immediately put his thumb on the red button and pushed.

The explosion sounded a lot like a shotgun going off, and the base of the tree suddenly seemed to disintegrate into a cloud of dust and dirt. As far away as they were, specks of dirt and tiny splinters of wood managed to hit them, though without any real force. The tree itself stood for a couple of seconds, and then slowly leaned to one side and fell.

"Tim-berrrr!" Neil yelled, his face covered in a massive grin. "Boss man," he said, "that stuff is awesome!"

Moose had gone by his house and packed up some clothes for the mission, also picking up the special Glock automatic that was the twin of one that Noah carried. It was another of Wally's team's creations, matched wirelessly with a ring that Moose wore on his right hand, and would not fire at all unless the hand holding it was wearing that ring.

Should anyone try to fire the gun without it, a high-voltage charge would be delivered through the grip, more powerful than a commercial stun gun. That person would be completely incapacitated for several minutes. They had not yet run into a situation where it was helpful, but both Noah and Moose agreed that it was a great tool for people in their line of work.

It was almost lunchtime, so Noah suggested they all go out for a bite to eat. They piled into the Chrysler, and Sarah took the wheel.

"Sagebrush?" she asked, and everyone agreed. She wheeled the sedan gently out of the driveway and then floored it. The car leaped forward, pressing everyone back into their seats.

"Good Lord, girl," Moose said from the backseat. "Lead foot, much?"

"Hey, I have to get familiar with this machine. You never know, I may have to pick you two up out of a bad situation. You wouldn't want me to be learning how to drive it in the middle of a firefight, now, would you?"

The in-dash GPS showed a scrolling view of the road, with a bright blue triangle representing the car. The curves in the road seemed a lot sharper on the little video display, and the rapidly moving triangle made it seem like they were going even faster than they probably really were. It seemed like only seconds before they came to the end of the country lane, and then they were on Temple Lake Road. It was just a few miles to the Sagebrush Saloon, but they were very curvy miles. Sarah put the car through its paces, and commented that the all-wheel drive and traction-grip tires made it seem like they were running on rails.

"I don't think so," Neil yelled. "The freaking tires are screaming around these curves, I don't think anything on rails would do that. Would you please slow down? We have enough chances to get killed when we're out on a mission, we don't need to risk it running around here at home!"

"Oh, poor baby," Sarah said, "am I scaring you?" She dropped her speed back down to the limit and drove sedately the rest of the way. When they got out of the car in the Saloon's parking lot, she actually patted it on the roof. "I could get used to driving something like this all the time."

Moose and Neil shook their heads and just walked past her into the restaurant. Noah stood at the front of the car and waited for a moment, then the two of them walked in together.

Elaine Jefferson, Moose's girlfriend, was working that afternoon and happily led them to one of her tables. She knew them all quite well and went to fetch their usual drinks while they thought about what to order for lunch. They had just gotten their orders in when Neil's cell phone rang.

He glanced at the caller ID display and broke into a huge smile, then got up and left the table while he answered the call.

"Must be Lacey," Sarah said. Lacey Jackson, who happened to be the daughter of their physical fitness instructor and was almost as tall and thin as the six-foot-five Neil, had introduced herself to him in the Saloon a few weeks before and they had become quite involved. It wasn't uncommon to see Lacey's car parked over at the trailer in the mornings. "She's been pretty good for him. Notice he's growing up a little bit, lately?"

"Neil? Growing up?" Moose asked, then looked over at Noah. "What kind of dope is she smoking lately? That kid ain't never gonna grow up."

Noah shrugged. "Actually, I think he's been a lot better lately. He doesn't whine nearly as much as he used to."

"Yes, he does," Moose said. "It just seems like it's not as much because he isn't constantly complaining about not having a girlfriend. Now he spends all his time complaining about not getting to spend enough time with his girlfriend."

"Which proves my point," Sarah said.

Moose shook his head. "Yeah, yeah, you keep on believing whatever you want to. Trust me, he's still a whiner."

"Yeah, maybe so, but you love him. You proved that when you took a bullet dragging him out of the line of fire, remember?"

"I never said I didn't," Moose said with a grin. "He's like the annoying little brother I never had. I always wanted one, just so I could pick on him, but Mom and Dad wouldn't cooperate. Now I got Neil, I'm making up for lost time."

Neil came back to the table just then, still smiling. "You guys don't mind if Lacey comes out to join us, do you? She went by the trailer and I wasn't home, so she called to see where I was."

"Oh-oh," Moose said. "When a girl gets to the point she's checking up to see where you are when you're not home, things must be getting pretty serious. Next thing you know, you'll have to ask for her permission to go on a mission with us." He put on an effeminate grin and tried to imitate Lacey's voice. "Okay, honey, you can go. Here's your balls, just make sure you get them back to me when you get home."

Neil gave him a sneer and stuck out his tongue. "Lacey isn't like that," he said. "She really cares about me, that's all."

Sarah watched the exchange with her eyes wide, then looked at Moose. "You're right, I take it back."

"Take what back?" Neil demanded.

"She just got through trying to tell me you had grown up since you started dating Lacey," Moose said. "I said you hadn't, and sticking your tongue out at me just proved my point."

Moose caught Elaine's attention and waved her over. "Honey, Lacey's gonna be joining us. Can we get another chair over here?"

Lacey arrived a little more than ten minutes later and took her seat beside Neil. She leaned over to give him a kiss and Neil blushed. "Hey, sweetie," she said, and then she looked at the rest of them. "Hope I'm not intruding."

"You're not," Sarah said, "and now that you're here, I don't feel quite as surrounded by testosterone as I did a minute ago. Thanks for coming."

"De nada, Chica," Lacey said. "Thanks for letting me barge in."

Elaine showed up only a few seconds later carrying a large tray and a folding stand. She flipped the stand open and set the tray on top, then begin passing out their orders. "Lacey, almost every time you come in here with Neil, you order the same thing he does. I hope it's okay, I went ahead and gave you an Italian beef like his."

Lacey smiled at her, delighted. "That's perfect," she said. "Thank you."

They dug in to eat, talking about inconsequential things. While Lacey and Elaine were privy to the type of work the team did, both of them being the daughters of top E & E people, most of the customers of the Saloon were simply local folk who knew nothing. As a result, mission work was rarely discussed there, and only when they were certain they could not be overheard.

Noah had already told his team that he was planning for them to leave for Missouri the following morning, so they decided to just hang out and relax for a while at the Saloon. It was nearly four o'clock by the time they finally left, and Neil rode home with Lacey rather than get back into the Chrysler with Sarah driving. Sarah kept the car under control, however, and her lead foot as well.

Lacey stayed right behind her all the way, and they all ended up at Noah's house.

When they turned onto the county lane, Sarah quickly reached down and pushed one of the color buttons while Lacey was out of sight. When they pulled up at the house and got out, she barely managed to keep from laughing when she saw Lacey staring at the now-red car.

Neil hurried Lacey inside to see the printer, but Noah refused to allow another demonstration of what it could do. Despite a short and mostly friendly argument, he refused to budge, so Neil took her out to see the remains of the tree.

Sarah looked at Noah. "You okay?"

"Yeah," he said. "It's just interesting, watching Neil trying to grow up. I'm seeing things in his behavior that I've never noticed before in other people."

"That's because," Sarah said with a chuckle, "you've never had to deal with an insecure teenager before. Neil has been lonely and scared most of his life, I think, partly because of how tall he is. People expect a tall guy like that to be athletic, but Neil never quite made it. It's probably made him self-conscious."

Noah nodded his head. "Yeah, that's what I'm seeing. It's interesting."

Lacey hung around with them for a couple of hours, but then Noah suggested it was time for her to head home. He had come up with a mission plan and it was time for him to go over it with the team. Neil walked her out and kissed her goodbye, then came back in with a long face and took his seat at the table.

"Okay, here's what I'm planning," Noah said. "We're going to spend a few days playing flower delivery. Neil, your job is going to be making sure we have accurate location intel on each of the targets, then using the printer to turn out flowerpots and vases. We'll want a lot of different designs, don't want them all to be exactly the same or that might arouse suspicion."

Neil nodded. "Okay, I'll try to learn everything I can about the targets, so that I can sort of gear the designs toward what they might like."

"Smart thinking," Noah said. He turned to Moose. "Moose, you will be on flower duty. I'll send you out to other cities in the area, like Jefferson City or Springfield, to buy flowers and plants and potting soil, stuff like that."

"Got it," Moose said.

"Sarah, you and I will be scouting. I want to get an eyeball on every target, and particularly on those two little kids. I've got to figure out a way to get them out of the line of fire and I'm not sure how to go about that just yet."

"Okay," Sarah said.

"Now, I don't want the van to be seen around the hotel, so we need to find someplace to use as a base of operations. Neil, see what you can come up with. If you can arrange for us to have a building somewhere by the time we get there, that would be great."

"Shouldn't be a problem," Neil said. He took out his phone and began poking at it. "Just scanning over Craigslist for that area, I can see quite a few possibilities. There's an old warehouse building in an industrial park. The rent isn't too bad, not that we really care about that. Privately owned—want me to call them now?"

Noah nodded. "Yes, go ahead. It would be good if we could have it ready to go into tomorrow night, when we get there."

THREE

The team pulled out the following morning at six AM with Noah and Sarah in the sedan, while Moose drove the van with Neil as his passenger. Despite all of Moose's semi-serious complaints about Neil, it was obvious to everyone who knew them that he really had adopted the skinny kid as a surrogate brother. The two of them often hung out together when they were between missions, and had already taken their respective girlfriends on double dates.

The trip to Columbia was almost a straight shot across Interstate 70, after an hour's driving on Colorado Route 71. They stopped for lunch in a little Kansas town near Salina, grabbing cheeseburgers and getting back on the road almost immediately, and didn't stop again until they hit Kansas City. They were all ready for a break by that time, so they stopped for a decent dinner and finally made it to Columbia at just before seven PM.

Neil had made the deal to rent the warehouse building, paying the first month's rent and deposit with a credit card over the phone the night before. The keys would be in a lock box that used a digital code, so they went straight to it when they arrived.

It wasn't a bad warehouse, but the little industrial park it sat in had seen better days. Most of the buildings were empty, so no one paid the four of them any attention as they collected the keys and parked the van inside. There were a number of workbenches scattered around there, and Neil commandeered one for the printer. Moose carried it over and set it up for him, and then they locked the building up again and went to find a hotel.

There was a decent one only a couple of miles away, and Noah decided it would work. Neil and Moose would share a room, as would Noah and Sarah, so he rented two for a week. They all gathered in his room and Sarah went to fetch soft drinks and snacks.

"We'll operate out of the warehouse," Noah said. "The less we're actually seen around the hotel, here, the better off we'll be. Everybody get a good night's sleep, I want to be up and out of here bright and early in the morning."

"Hey," Neil said, "I saw a Denny's down the road. Can we go there for breakfast?"

"That sounds okay. Let's just relax for the night and get some rest, because tomorrow the mission really begins."

Moose and Neil said goodnight and headed for their room, and Sarah went to the bathroom to take a shower. Noah sat back on the bed and turned on the television in the room, flipping through channels to look for something worth watching. He found the channel guide and spotted a movie that looked interesting, one that would be starting in a short time, so he waited until Sarah came out of the shower and then went to get his own.

The movie was starting as he came back out of the bathroom, so he and Sarah bunched up their pillows and sat on the bed to watch. She leaned against him, and he put his arm around her to hold her close. As the movie was beginning, he noticed her looking up at his face.

"What's up?"

Sarah shrugged. "Just enjoying this," she said. "You've been—I don't know, more cuddly lately? I like it, but I can't help wondering why."

Noah sat for a moment and thought about how to answer, then leaned over and kissed the top of her head. "I could just tell you that holding you close to me gives me a pleasant sensation," he said. "I can tell you that I do it because I think you need it. Both of those have some truth to them, so I wouldn't be lying." He paused and leaned his head back against the wall behind it. "The truth is, I'm not really sure why I'm doing it. I've come to realize that I like having you close to me, and that's something I'm not accustomed to."

Sarah was quiet for a moment, and Noah waited for her to speak. "One of the reasons Allison wanted you was because you don't have any emotional attachments. If you—if you are starting to have some kind of feelings for me, is that going to interfere? Is it going to make it harder for you to do your job?"

Noah shook his head. "No," he said. "I don't see why it would."

Sarah sat up and leaned against the wall so that she could look straight at his face. "Noah, we haven't talked about it, but you know you broke the rules when you came to rescue me. We're all expendable, remember? I think Allison is afraid that our relationship is going to cause a problem."

"I disagree. My mission at that time was to locate Nicolaich Andropov, and he had you. From a strictly logical standpoint, you could say that I didn't come to rescue you, I came to try to kill him. Bringing you out alive was simply a bonus."

"Remember the debriefing? You told Jefferson that you came after me because you didn't like the idea of the world not having me in it anymore. In absolutely anybody else, that would be a sign of love. With you, I'm just not sure what it means, but I'll happily take what I can get."

Noah lowered his eyebrows, and then turned to face her. "I read a book once, a long time ago. One of the characters was trying to define what love means, and I always liked his definition. He said that love was the condition that exists whenever another person's happiness and well-being is necessary for your own happiness and well-being." He chewed his bottom lip for a few seconds. "I don't have a clue what it feels like to be in love, but if we look at that definition and accept it, then I guess we can say that I love you. I like it when you smile, I like it when you laugh—I don't like it when you're hurt or unhappy. It seems to me that your happiness and well-being are essential to whatever equivalent of those I might have, so that fits."

Sarah stared at him for a moment, then smiled. "I love you too, you big jerk," she said, and then she leaned against him again as they watched the movie. When it ended, they slid down into the bed and found other ways to express how much they enjoyed being together.

By six thirty the next morning, they were all up and ready to go. Noah opened the door to find Moose and Neil just about to knock, so they all went to the car together. Denny's, as Neil had said, was only a short distance away. Sarah pulled in and parked and they all filed inside for breakfast.

They spent an hour over pancakes and sausage and eggs and coffee, then got back into the car and headed for the warehouse. Neil had brought his own computer along, and set it up on another table near the 3-D printer, along with his own portable inkjet printer and a police scanner. He laid his copy of the target files beside it and began studying the individuals in the file.

Alejandra Gomez and her husband Enrique were first. While both of them were involved in the cartel, it was Alejandra, the youngest member of the branch, who seemed to be in charge of the group in Columbia. According to the limited intelligence that had been gathered on them, Alejandra called all the shots. This made her, of course, Noah's number one target, with her husband and other family members on the list simply because of their association with her.

Eduardo Menendez was a widower, but he had three of his sons and two of his brothers living with him. All of them were actively involved, and he was number two on the list.

Ramon Hernandez was next. Besides his wife and one adult son, he was accompanied by two uncles and their wives. All of them were deeply entrenched in the cartel, and Ramon was number three.

Armando Rodriguez seemed to be the man who dealt most with the dealers, and his two brothers and an uncle represented the muscle in his organization. While all of the cartel members were involved in various aspects of the drug business, it was the Rodriguez group who tended to hand out discipline. Usually, it came in the form of beatings, but several people had been obviously executed.

Last, but far from least, was Carlos Perez. Carlos, along with his wife and two daughters, handled the business end of their venture. Mrs. Perez was an accountant, and reportedly kept track of the many millions of dollars that flowed through their branch. Their daughters assisted her, but it was rumored that they had been involved in a couple of murders, using feminine charms to lure at least two men to their deaths.

The home addresses of each of them had been provided, along with a list of each and every occupant. Neil began looking for ways to spy on them, and it didn't take him long to discover that all of the homes were clients of a single local security company. An hour later, he had hacked his way into its security video server and could watch in real time as people entered and left.

Noah sat beside him as he went over what he was seeing.

"This is the Gomez household," Neil said. "They've got security cameras on every entrance, and several around the yard. I can get a complete, three hundred and sixty-degree view of the house and grounds."

"But there aren't any cameras inside?" Noah asked.

"Afraid not, Boss. On the other hand, they're using a standard cable company Wi-Fi system. When I get into it, I should be able to access any web cams inside the house. That might give you some internal views."

"That would be good, if you can. What about the security alarms?"

"I got access to the company's main servers," Neil said. "I can turn off the alarms, either altogether or just by disabling one door or window."

Noah nodded. "Good, that may come in handy. I need to figure out a way to get those two children out of the house before we do anything."

"Um, on that," Neil said. "Turns out Mrs. Gomez has a nanny, a local lady she hired through a service. I noticed in the file that it mentioned her, so I'm wondering if maybe she takes the kids out, sometimes. Maybe she takes them to the park or something, you know what I mean?"

"Good thinking. Try to find out for me, will you?"

They went over the security video from the other houses, but just seeing the outsides didn't help a lot. "I wonder if there's any kind of recorded blueprints for those houses," Noah mused aloud. "I'd really like to have some idea of the interior layouts. I want to get these bombs in there, but I want to make sure they get the job done."

Neil cocked his head and grimaced. "I'll do what I can," he said. "Maybe I can find out who built the houses. If it was a development company, they might have blueprints stored somewhere digitally that I can crack into. Don't get your hopes up, though."

"I understand, just do what you can," Noah said. "What about the neighborhood? How close are the other houses?"

"Gomez lives in what looks like a pretty expensive neighborhood," Neil replied. "From what I can see from the security cameras, the Gomez house probably sits on a couple of acres, at least. It's at least a hundred yards to the nearest house on either side. Some of the others live not far away, but the Perez family is all the way across the city."

Moose had left a few minutes earlier, heading to Jefferson City in the van to begin buying up flowers, so Noah left Neil to his work as he and Sarah went to scout the area. He had programmed all of the addresses of the houses into the GPS in the dash, and it took them only a couple of hours to locate and drive by all of them. Sarah cut through alleys and changed the color of the car between each one, so no one would notice the same car driving by more than one of them.

"If you're going to use the explosives," she asked at one point, "why are you looking the houses over so hard?"

"The explosives are good," Noah said, "but in order to do their jobs, they need to be placed where they'll have the most devastating effect on the structure. If I set one off and it only takes out part of one room, then at least some of the targets are likely to survive. We got five locations to deal with, so I can't be everywhere at once. When the bombs go off, I need to be as sure as I possibly can that they get the job done."

"That sounds like you need more than one bomb in each house. How do you plan to accomplish that?"

"Well, we can simply deliver a lot of flowers," Noah said. "Or we can give them something that's big enough that when it goes off, there won't be any part of the house left standing. That's what I've got to figure out. Then there's the problem of giving them things they'll accept. We can't just deliver flowers without saying who they're from or what they're for."

Sarah drove in silence for a few minutes, then looked over at Noah. "When my dad did a one-year stint in the federal prison," she said, "one of the things he told me was that almost all of the Mexican inmates were part of this cult, something called the Holy

Death. From the way he made it sound, just about every drug dealer in the Hispanic world worships death. I wonder if these people do."

Noah looked over at her. "I've heard of that, it's called Santa Muerte. Some of the guys in my unit in the Army were into it." He reached into his pocket and took out his phone. "Neil? See if you can find out if any of these people are into the Santa Muerte religion."

"Santa Muerte? If my Spanish is any good, and I know it is, that translates to holy death?"

"Yeah, they actually worship Death, like it's some kind of a saint. They pray to it, asking for favors, all kinds of stuff. Let me know what you find out." He ended the call and turned to Sarah again. "Holy Death followers tend to keep an altar. The guys I knew in the Army, they kept theirs in their lockers. Some of them were pretty complicated."

Sarah nodded. "Yeah, that's what Dad said. They kept a statue, a skeleton in a long dress, and had all kinds of things around it."

"Right. We might be able to use that." He glanced at his phone and checked the time. "It's almost lunchtime," he said. "How about we pick up some tacos and head back?"

"Sounds good to me," Sarah said. "I know we had breakfast, but I'm still kind of hungry. Look, there's a taco stand right up the street. One of the benefits of being in a Mexican neighborhood, I guess."

Moose was back by the time they arrived at the warehouse, but Noah had anticipated it. They had brought back plenty of tacos, nachos and burritos for everyone, and Neil told Noah what he had learned as they ate.

"This Holy Death thing, it's really weird," the skinny kid said. "From what I've been able to learn, a lot of people involved in the drug trade are into it. They pray to this skeletal figure in a long dress, kinda looks like a wedding dress, and they ask her to keep them safe from the police. The weird thing is, they'd rather get killed than arrested. I guess they believe that if they get killed while they're working at the drug trade, it gets them some kind of special spot in Heaven."

"That sounds about right," Noah said. "I've known guys in the Army who were into it, and that were convinced that if they died on patrol they'd go straight to paradise."

Neil nodded his head. "Yeah, exactly. Well, all of these people seem to be into it, according to the DEA. If their intel is correct, each of those houses has several small shrines in it."

Noah pursed his lips in thought. "Hmmm," he said. "That might not be much help, after all. If they've already got shrines…"

"Don't jump so fast," Neil said. "I stumbled across one thing that you might find pretty interesting. About three months ago, one of Armando Rodriguez's brothers was killed. Guess what happened right after that."

Noah shook his head. "No guess, just tell me."

"The whole freaking bunch of them, I mean all of them, every aunt, uncle, cousin, brother, sister, the whole bunch, they all showed up at Alejandra's place. They gathered there to pray to Saint Holy Death for the dead guy to get a special place in Heaven, since he was killed in a drug robbery that went bad."

Noah sat and looked at him for a long moment, then began chewing his lip again. "So, if something happens that they consider an emotional blow to the entire group, they all get together in one place?"

"If it's something they need to pray to Little Miss Skeleton about, then that's a pretty safe bet. Now, the DEA says they have a bunch of these little altars, right? Well, from what I read online, they like to worship at the biggest shrine they can find. I bet you can figure out what's going through my mind, can't you?"

Noah cocked his head to the side, and actually grinned. "Yeah," he said. "You're thinking the same thing I am. We need to make a fair-sized shrine to this thing and give it as a gift to one of our targets, and then give them a reason to hold a prayer meeting."

Neil was smiling and nodding. "Exactly," he said. "I'll get started on a design for the shrine right away, okay, Boss?"

"That'll be perfect. All I've got to do now is come up with a good reason for delivering it to them."

FOUR

It was Sarah who discovered a solution to Noah's dilemma that afternoon, as they worked at the warehouse. Intrigued by the entire concept of the Holy Death cult, she had begun googling it out of curiosity, and that led her to stumble across the Wikipedia page that was dedicated to it. On that page, she learned that one of the most famous shrines to Santa Muerte had been a gift, one that a man gave to his mother as a way of thanking the folk saint for the fact that he had been rapidly released from jail after an arrest.

She pointed it out to Noah. "I was thinking about this, and it hit me that it might be the answer. What if you said it was sent by one of their people who had gotten arrested, like part of a prayer to keep them out of prison? They'd probably accept it without a problem, then, right?"

"That's an excellent idea," Noah said. He turned to Neil. "Can you get a list of their dealers that have been locked up? See if you can find one who's looking at a long sentence."

"I'm on it," Neil replied. He tapped on the keys for a few moments, then held one finger pointed up toward the sky. "Bingo! Duane Harris, arrested about two months ago, prosecutors say he's looking at sixty years. And get this, local newspaper made a big issue over a Holy Death shrine in his living room when he was arrested. Apparently the local churches are throwing real fits about this cult coming into their city."

Noah nodded. "Sounds like our patsy," he said. He turned and looked at Moose, who was repotting flowers into the new pots the printer was turning out. Neil had found several flowerpot designs already loaded into the printer's database, and Noah had shown Moose how to program the detonators. Noah watched him for a moment, then turned to Neil again. "Let's stop at about a dozen floral arrangements, then get busy on the shrine. I think a life-size one might be a bit too grandiose, and probably pretty expensive for your average drug dealer. Let's go for one about four or five feet tall, one that looks like it had some effort put into it, but isn't quite perfect."

"Making the skeleton isn't the problem," Neil said. "I found a design in the 3-D image database that's built into the printer controller, and I can make it as big or small as we want. The real issue is going to be the way it's dressed. They dress them in different colors for different things they're praying for, but we have to make sure it looks realistic to one of the devoted followers of the cult."

"Right," Sarah said. "The question is, what color would she be wearing for a family crisis? I mean, you want to get the whole family together to pray to this thing, right?"

"Yes, but you're getting ahead of yourself," Noah said. "We don't need to worry about how she would be dressed for that. We just need to think about how she would be dressed when she gets delivered. What would be the most common color for her to wear?"

"White," Moose said from where he was working. "I got curious about it, too, so I googled it. When they're asking for something, they usually put her in white."

"Okay, then the next question is where do we get something appropriate to dress it in. Any suggestions?"

"That's easy," Sarah said. "You want white? Get a wedding dress. You can probably find one small enough for what you want in a costume shop. Order it online and pay for overnight shipping, you'd have it tomorrow."

Neil opened another browser and started tapping on the keyboard. "She's right, there's plenty of them. White satin, complete with veil and everything."

Noah leaned forward and looked at the picture on the monitor. "If you think it'll work, go ahead and order it. Get it here by tomorrow if you can, so we can start getting this put together."

Neil put in the order while Sarah went to help Moose with the flowerpots. As soon as she was out of earshot, Noah leaned close to Neil again.

"So, what have you learned about the nanny?"

Neil turned to face him with a grimace. "Unfortunately, not a lot so far. I'm keeping an eye on the security cameras, trying to get an idea of when she might leave the house with the kids. No luck so far. You would have thought the DEA might have paid attention to little details like that, but no, they couldn't be bothered."

"Keep watching. We want to give them all something to get together about, and I can't think of anything more likely to do it than for those two kids to get snatched. We get them out of harm's way and force a gathering of the cartel members in town in a single shot. I think it's our best move."

"Yeah," Neil said, nodding his head. "Just hope your girlfriend is up for it. She seemed pretty upset when the Dragon Lady mentioned those two little ones."

"That's because she wasn't sure whether I'd actually kill them or not," Noah said. "She doesn't want them to get hurt, of course, so she knows this is the best way to handle it. Don't worry about her, she'll do what I need her to do."

He got up and walked over to look at the floral arrangements that were coming together. Moose had been smart enough to buy extra accessories, like ribbons and little plastic sticks that hold a card, as well as a selection of cards themselves. Noah's plan was to deliver the Santa Muerte shrine as soon as possible, and then abduct Alejandra Gomez's two toddlers the next day. The cartel members would almost certainly think it was related to their drug business, so it was a safe bet that they would not approach the police for help. They would be far more likely to try to find the perpetrators on their own so that they could deliver their own brand of justice. For that reason, they would gather both to talk about the problem and to pray for the children's safe return. He was betting that they would gather at the new, bigger shrine.

Once the abduction was accomplished, Neil would watch the security cameras in order to see when the members began to gather. If there was a delay, Moose would begin delivering flowers to them, expressions of sympathy from acquaintances. Noah even planned to order flowers from other local florists, just so that no one would get suspicious about the same van coming and going all the time.

Noah and Sarah would handle the abduction, and they had already prepared a room in the warehouse as a temporary place to keep the nanny and children. They would go out sometime the next day to scour the thrift shops for cribs and a bed, then stock up on diapers, baby food and other necessities until a pair of specialists from another branch of E & E arrived to take charge of them. The children would be placed with an adoption agency in another state, and the nanny would be released unharmed in yet another after the mission was complete.

Neil would be in charge of keeping them under guard until they were retrieved, with Moose to relieve him periodically. That would allow Noah and Sarah to keep moving, while staying close to the Gomez home. They would be waiting for word from Neil that the gathering had begun, and as soon as they were sure that at least a majority of the targets were inside, Sarah would bring Noah close enough for the detonator remote to work. All of the detonators were programmed to channel 7, so the shrine and flowerpots would all explode at once. There should be enough explosive within the house to level it completely and shred everyone inside.

Sarah glanced at him, and for a split second Noah wondered if she was reading his mind. He knew she was worried about the children, about the unavoidable trauma they would suffer after being kidnapped and losing their families, but there was simply no way to completely protect them from it. These children were innocent, and would probably be raised by a new family without ever knowing their true history. It was the best Noah could do for them.

"You okay?" Noah asked, and she shrugged her shoulders, but with a grin on her face.

"I guess so," she said. "You know, all those years when I was growing up, I didn't ever really think about the fact I was helping my dad steal cars. I always thought of myself as a pretty good kid, you know what I mean? If someone had told me even three years ago that I would one day be helping to make bombs to kill a bunch of drug dealers, I would've said they were crazy." She rolled her eyes. "Now look at me. I'm so deeply entrenched into this, now, I'm not only part of an assassination team, I'm in love with a man who kills people for a living. It's not exactly the Cinderella, happily-ever-after kind of thing that most girls dream about, you know?"

"I can imagine," Noah said. "Let's face it, I'm not any kind of Prince Charming, anyway." He looked at Moose. "How's it coming?"

"Better, now that Sarah is helping me out. I can stuff potting soil in a pot, stick flowers in there all day long, but I just don't have the eye to make it look like something pretty. She does. With her helping, people might actually believe these came from a real flower shop."

"Good, we need this to look as realistic as possible." Noah glanced at his phone to check the time. "It's almost five thirty," he said. "Anybody hungry?"

They all admitted that they could eat, so Noah sent Sarah out to pick up sandwiches, fries and drinks. She was back within half an hour, and they took a break to have dinner. By the time they were finished, the last flowerpot had been taken out of the printer. All four of them worked together to finish the last four floral arrangements, with Sarah advising them all.

"Okay, let's make us a skeleton," Neil said.

The skeleton would have to be assembled, with each section printed out separately. The feet, shins, thighs, pelvis, spine, rib cage, shoulder blades, upper arms, forearms, hands, neck bones, skull and lower jaw were each individual designs. He called up the feet on the monitor, and set it to printing the right one first.

Each section would require a separate detonator, so there were a total of twenty of them involved. As fast as the printer was, it still took over four hours to make all of the parts, including a rod to help it stand up, and then they had to be snapped together. Luckily, they had been designed for easy assembly, but it was still almost 11 o'clock before the entire four-foot skeleton was laid out on the table.

They were as prepared as they could be up to that point. All that remained was to wait for the dress to arrive the next day and gather up a supply of jewelry with which to decorate the shrine.

"All right, let's go get some rest," Noah said. "Tomorrow morning, Sarah, you can run out and see what kind of jewelry you can find."

"From what I see online," Neil said, "it doesn't have to be expensive stuff. Old costume jewelry would work just fine—the shinier and flashier, the better."

"That ought to be easy. I can hit some of the thrift stores, they usually have lots of that kind of stuff. Salvation Army, here I come!"

When they got to the hotel, they said goodnight and went to their rooms. Sarah waited until they had gotten inside before she turned and put her arms around Noah's neck, pulling him down for a kiss.

"Well," Noah said, "what did I do to deserve that?"

"Nothing yet," Sarah said with a mischievous grin. "It's what you're about to do." She peeled his shirt off over his head and reached for the buckle of his belt. "I'll explain the rest when we get in the shower."

* * * * *

Noah had told them they could all sleep in a bit the next morning, but old habits are hard to break. By seven thirty, they were all awake and ready for breakfast. The hotel had a waffle maker and other items for a free breakfast, so they decided to simply eat there.

"Waffles," Neil said, "are one of God's great gifts to mankind."

"You say that about every kind of food," Sarah said, poking him in the ribs. "As much as you eat, I cannot understand how on earth you can stay so skinny."

"Hey! Stop that!" Neil said, slapping at her hand. "I can't help it I'm still growing."

"If you're still growing, kid," Moose said, "then you're going to have a big problem. You can barely get through a doorway now."

Neil sneered at him. "Yeah? How's the weather down there, Shorty?"

The easy banter continued while they ate, but then it was time to get to work, so they cleaned up after themselves and went out to the car. Sarah dropped the three men off at the warehouse, then went in search of jewelry and baby needs.

One of the things she had been told over and over during her training for E & E was to avoid drawing attention to herself during a mission. Regardless of what kind of vehicle she was driving, she was always supposed to keep it under the speed limit, signal every turn, do everything by the book so that no one would take any notice of her or the car.

Normally, that wasn't a problem, but when she came to the first stoplight, she found herself right beside two young men in a brand-new Corvette, and the driver kept looking over at her with a grin while revving his engine. She smiled at him, but that only encouraged him. He rolled down his window and began calling for her to race him to the next light.

Sarah shook her head, still smiling, but the boy didn't give up easily. His friend was making faces at her, and clucking noises, and she suddenly found it annoying. She glanced at the rearview mirror, then looked all around to see if there were likely to be any police in the area.

She saw nothing, so she turned and glanced at the Corvette's driver again, then winked. He broke out into a huge smile, and revved the engine a couple more times as they waited for the light to turn green.

Green appeared, and the rear tires of the Corvette suddenly began spinning and screaming, as the driver gave it all he had. Sarah shook her head at his foolishness and pushed her own foot to the floor. The Chrysler's all-wheel drive grabbed the road and threw her forward like a rocket, leaving the Corvette sitting in a cloud of its own black smoke.

It was almost a quarter of a mile to the next light, and Sarah had been sitting stopped at it for more than five seconds before the Corvette pulled up beside her. The driver was staring at her in awe, but his comments and taunts had come to an end. The passenger was looking straight ahead, unwilling to even turn his eyes in her direction.

When the light changed again, Sarah drove away sedately. The young driver of the Corvette gave his car more accelerator and pulled quickly away, but Sarah knew that he would never forget the day a big four-door sedan had left him sitting still at the light.

Three hours later, with three big bags of costume jewelry, Sarah returned to the warehouse. She dumped it all out on the table, and she and Neil began choosing the items they would use to decorate the shrine. She had bought necklaces, bracelets, brooches and more, all kinds of sparkly, shiny things to represent the offerings believers would present to Santa Muerte.

She sent Moose out to the car to get her other purchases. Two folding cribs, a playpen and a folding cot for an adult were carried in, followed by a TV, a mini fridge and plenty of snacks and soft drinks to stock it with. There were also three big bags of diapers, baby food and other necessities. Moose set them all in the room they had set aside as a holding area for the nanny and babies, and then he and Neil began setting them up.

And then they waited. According to the tracking number Neil had gotten via email, the dress was scheduled to arrive sometime in the afternoon. There wasn't a lot they could do until then, so Noah went over the plan with them one more time.

"Once the skeleton is dressed and ready, Moose will load it into the van and take it to the Gomez house. We'll put a card with it that indicates it was a gift from a friend of Duane Harris, asking them to pray for his release. Once they have accepted it and taken it inside, that's when we'll start watching for the nanny to take the children out. Immediately after that, Moose, you're going to go and steal us a car, something big but not too noticeable. Sarah and I will use that car to go and find the nanny and children, forcing them into the car and bringing them back here. Hopefully, we can do that without drawing any attention, but we'll stay away from the warehouse until we're sure we're not being followed. At that point, we'll need you to bring the Chrysler and pick us up somewhere, Moose. We don't want the stolen car connected to this location."

"Right," Moose said, "I'll be ready."

"Noah," Sarah said, "why don't we just use the Chrysler? I can flip the plates and change the color, so no one would know it was the same car we're driving now."

Noah shook his head. "No, we don't want to overuse what that car can do unless we absolutely have to. That's a pretty powerful feature, and I can see how it could save our asses if we need it, but the last thing we need is someone saying they saw a car like that changing color as it went down the road. For this purpose, it's better to use a completely different car."

"Okay, I can see your point. I'm just dying to use it."

"Hang on, and I'm sure you'll get the chance sooner or later. Neil, when Moose leaves to come pick us up, I want you to call the Gomez house and use one of your computerized voices to deliver the message in Spanish that the kids have been kidnapped, and that we want ten million dollars in ransom. Tell them that we'll be back in touch with instructions, then cut the call off. That should start the ball rolling."

"Not a problem," Neil said. "My Spanish is pretty good, and the computer can make me sound like somebody from their neck of the woods."

"Good. As soon as we get the nanny and kids locked away here, I'll notify Queen Allison that they're ready for pickup. We'll wait about three hours after the abduction, give it time to let the news spread about it, and if nothing is happening, then the first load of flowers can be delivered. Neil, you be sure to use a similar voice to order flowers from two or three other flower shops around town, get them delivered as quickly as possible to the Gomez house. An hour or so later, Moose, you can take the last batch of flowers to them."

"Got it, Boss."

"Sarah, once we drop the nanny and kids off here, we get into the car and just start circling around that area of the city. The idea is to be as close as possible when the gathering begins. Neil, you'll be keeping tabs on who's going in and out of that house, I want to get as many of them as possible inside. If we miss any, Moose and I will have to track them down and take them out one by one."

"They all got together when that one guy was killed," Neil said, "so I figure they'll do it again over Mrs. Gomez losing her kids. They're all supposed to be pretty close, so it would make sense."

Noah nodded in agreement. "I think you're right, but we have to prepare for contingencies. Keep your eye on as many of those cameras as you can, I need to know about any of the targets who manage not to get caught in the trap."

"Will do."

FIVE

The day dragged on, but finally a big brown delivery truck appeared. Noah had put Sarah at the reception desk in the front office of the warehouse, and she smiled at the driver as he carried a box inside.

"Is this Avalon Floral?"

"It sure is," Sarah said cheerfully. "Got something for me?"

The driver smiled and set the box on the counter in front of her, then held out a device and asked her to use a stylus to sign for the package. She quickly scribbled "Rosemary Wingo" and handed it back. The driver smiled once more, winked at her and then headed back to his truck and drove away.

Sarah grabbed the box and headed out into the warehouse, where Moose took it from her and began to open it up. The wedding dress he lifted out of it was small, but very pretty.

"Wow," Sarah said, "that's pretty nice. If it was a little bigger, I could wear it."

Neil spun in his chair to look at her, his eyes wide. "You guys getting married?"

Sarah's eyes were suddenly even wider than his. "What? No! No, I just meant—I mean, I was just saying—oh, shut up, Neil!"

Moose started laughing. "I wish you could see your face, Sarah," he said. "I don't think I've ever seen you turn quite so red before."

"You shut up, too!"

"Okay, okay," Moose said. "You want to come help dress up Bony Girl? Even if you're not getting married, you probably know more about how to put on a wedding dress than we do."

Sarah stared at him blankly for a moment, then grinned. "Yeah, probably," she said. "I doubt any of you have ever been near one before now." She walked over to the table and began looking it over. "Remember, this is just a costume, it doesn't even fasten like a real wedding gown. It's got these three little hooks in the back instead of a zipper or buttons. Set the skeleton down on the floor, please?"

Moose did as she asked, and Sarah slid the dress down over its head, fumbling to get the bony arms into the sleeves without ripping the lace. It took her only a couple of minutes, and then she stood back and looked at it.

"Okay, let's get the jewelry on her." She began picking through the pile they had made the day before, adding different ornaments to the figure as she went along.

"We missed something," Neil said, "actually a couple of things. Santa Muerte is supposed to be holding a couple of objects, mainly a scythe—she's Death, right?—and a globe, like of the world. I guess that's supposed to mean she has the power of life and death over everything." He looked at Noah. "I can make them, with the printer. They should look okay that way."

Noah nodded. "Yes, go ahead. We need this to look as real as possible."

Neil nodded once and went to the printer. He couldn't find a scythe in the image database, but it took him only a few minutes to create one with the CAD software that was built into it, and the printer began working at its normal rapid pace.

Sarah was actually enjoying herself, and Noah cocked his head to one side as he watched her work. It took a moment, but she saw him.

"What?" Sarah asked.

Noah shook his head. "Just watching you," he said. "You were smiling, and it caught my attention."

Sarah blushed and looked away. "I was just remembering when I was a little girl, before my mom died. She used to buy me dolls, and we'd play dress up with them. I hadn't thought about that in a long time, but this reminded me of it."

Noah nodded. "I knew it was just you and your dad when you got busted and recruited, but I never knew what happened to your mother. How old were you when she died?"

"I was eleven," Sarah said. "It wasn't sudden. She got cancer, and we knew for a couple of years that it was coming, but it still hurt when she was gone."

Noah said nothing, and a moment later she went on. "After that, it was just me and my dad. I don't think he ever got over it, to be honest. He never dated or anything, always said he didn't have time for that kind of thing, but he was always ready to take me to the movies, or out to play putt-putt. If he hadn't taught me how to steal cars before I turned eleven, it would've been a pretty decent childhood."

She added a couple more pieces and stood back to look at her handiwork. "Not bad," she said. "Neil, what do you think?"

Neil walked over and looked at the figure, nodding his head. "Looks like the pictures I found online," he said. "When the scythe and globe get done, I'd say she's ready, Boss."

"Scythe looks like it's ready," Moose said. He reached into the printer and picked it up.

Neil had done a good job on it. The handle, properly curved, looked like wood, while the blade appeared to be made of steel. Only the weight made it clear that it was plastic. Moose carried it over and carefully bent the fingers of the skeletal right hand around it, but the arm wouldn't stay in position. Sarah rolled up the sleeve while Moose applied superglue to the elbow joint to lock it in place.

Neil started the printer on the globe. This time, he was able to find one in the database, one that showed all of the continents engraved into what appeared to be a silver ball. He turned the printer loose and it began working. Fifteen minutes later, the shiny four-inch globe was ready.

Moose and Sarah had gone ahead and prepared the left hand, bending and locking the elbow so that the hand was positioned just in front of where the skeleton's heart would be, if it had one. Another drop of superglue attached a silver chain from a necklace to the globe, and that was draped over the hand.

The four of them stood back and looked at their creation, and Neil let out a low whistle. "I gotta say, that looks pretty awesome to me. Don't get me wrong, I'm not ready to start praying to a bony bitch, but if I was one of her followers, I think I'd want one of these in my living room."

"We didn't think about a box," Noah said. "I don't think anybody would expect one of these to be delivered without being in some kind of a box."

Neil shrugged. "I wouldn't even know where to look for a box this size," he said. "Anybody got any ideas?"

Sarah nodded. "Yeah," she said. "Be right back." She turned and walked out the door, got into the car and drove away. She was gone about half an hour, and when she pulled up again she removed a large package from the back seat and carried it inside.

The package turned out to be a doll, one of the "Your Size" fashion dolls. The plastic girl inside was just barely taller than the skeleton they had made, and the front panel of the box was clear plastic.

"I had one of these when I was a kid," Sarah said. "I was pretty sure the big toy chains still sold them, and I was right. Our Santa Muerte will fit right inside, but we need to do something about the labeling on the box." She opened a bag that she had carried in with the box and pulled out a small can of gold paint and a couple of brushes.

Moose opened the box and removed the doll, and then he and Sarah began painting. The metallic gold paint covered the original lettering perfectly, and while it was obvious the box had been reused, it appeared to have been very nicely done.

Neil used his portable inkjet printer to create a banner that read, *"Gracias!"* and Sarah stuck it directly to the paint in the upper left corner, so that it crossed the corner of the clear panel at an angle. The paint dried quickly, but it was still after seven PM by the time they finally had the skeletal figure tucked inside and ready to go.

"I doubt any flower companies deliver at this time of night," Noah said, "so we'll be starting first thing in the morning. Let's go find some dinner and then get some rest."

Instead of going out to eat, they decided to pick up pizzas and take them back to the hotel. They gathered in Noah and Sarah's room and found a movie on the television, a fairly recent film from the new *Star Trek* series.

Neil pointed at the screen when Mr. Spock came on. "Look, Boss, you're on TV."

Noah looked at him and raised one eyebrow. "Fascinating," he said. "When I was a kid, one of my best friends introduced me to the old *Star Trek* TV show, and told me I was like Mr. Spock. I used to watch that show every chance I got, just to see how he put up with all those humans around him. Personally, I don't think this new guy does the character justice. Leonard Nimoy was Mr. Spock, and that's all there was to it."

The movie ended, Moose and Neil went off to their room, and Sarah dragged Noah into the bed. She cuddled up close to him and just lay there for a moment.

"What happens if the nanny doesn't cooperate and bring the kids out where we can grab them?"

Noah looked her in the eye. "If I have to, I'll go take them right out of the house. I'm not going to let them be there when those explosives go off, and we need the abduction to give the cartel members a reason to gather."

Sarah's head was lying on Noah's shoulder, and his right arm was around her. She rubbed her face on his shoulder and then looked up at him again. "I always get scared," she said, "the night before the mission gets heavy. This one sounds like it should come off pretty easy, but I'm not sure. We're adding in a kidnapping; that's like throwing lit matches into a box of firecrackers. Something's bound to blow up."

"We'll just have to play it by ear," Noah said. "I'm just counting on you to get us off the radar as quickly as possible after we have those kids. That's the only place where I see any real potential problems. If the local police were to get on our trail, things could get pretty messed up."

Sarah sighed into his shoulder. "Then just make sure Moose gets me something that can move. There's nothing I hate worse than running from cops in a vehicle that doesn't have the power or maneuverability it needs."

She tilted her face up for a kiss and Noah obliged her. A few moments later he heard her breathing slow as she drifted off to sleep. He relaxed and followed her after only a few more seconds.

They rose at six, showered and then went out for breakfast. Moose had spotted a place that looked appealing the day before, and it turned out to have a terrific breakfast menu. All four of them went for the steak and eggs, even Sarah moaning with delight as she bit into the T-bone.

They pulled up at the warehouse at eight AM on the dot and went inside to look the shrine over one more time. It was already in the box, so all they could do was look through the plastic window, but Noah finally nodded his approval.

"Okay, it's time to do this. Moose, you probably ought to have some flowers in the van with you, just in case anyone pays attention. It wouldn't do for them to remember a few days from now that some flower shop delivery van dropped off a box, but didn't have anything else inside."

Moose nodded and began loading some of their floral arrangements inside the van, then picked up the box and laid it carefully on the floor behind the front passenger seat. He climbed into the van as Neil pushed the button to open the overhead door, then backed it out, turned around and was gone.

"Neil, get on those cameras. I need a window of opportunity, either with the nanny taking the children out somewhere, or a definite time when she and the kids are there alone. Keep your eyes peeled and let me know the second you have something."

"I'm all over it," Neil said.

It was time to wait. Noah and Sarah sat together in the folding chairs beside Neil, watching the minutes pass by. It would take Moose about half an hour to get to the Gomez house, but nothing could happen until they saw the box taken inside.

Suddenly, Neil pointed at the monitor. "There's Moose," he said. "The van just pulled up in the driveway. No sign that anyone in the house has noticed him, yet." He paused for a couple of seconds, then said, "He just got out, he's walking around the van to get to the side door. Got it open, picked up the box—there he goes, up the driveway to the walk. Up the stairs, looks like he's ringing the doorbell. Okay, somebody just opened the door, looks like Mrs. Gomez herself. Moose is talking, she's smiling, and now she's looking into the box and smiling even bigger. Boss, I think we got a winner, here. Yep, she took the box inside, and there goes Moose. He's back in the van, backing out of the driveway and out of sight."

Less than a minute later, Noah's cell phone rang and he pulled it out of his pocket. "Go," he said as he answered. It was Moose calling, of course, letting them know that the first phase of the mission had gone off without a hitch. The high-explosive shrine was inside the house.

"Good job," Noah said. "Now go get us some wheels, and Sarah said to tell you to make sure it can move and handle."

"No problem, I got it all figured out. Meet me at the McDonald's by the mall in half an hour."

Noah agreed and put the phone away, then motioned for Sarah to follow him. "Get me something, Neil," Noah said. "We need to make this happen today."

"Sure, no problem, I'll just snap my fingers and make the nanny take the kids to the park. All in a day's work for the magic man, no big deal." He rolled his eyes as Noah and Sarah left the building. They pulled away in the Chrysler a moment later, and Neil began to concentrate on the monitor once again.

It took them almost the entire half hour to get to the rendezvous. Sarah parked the Chrysler at the back of the parking lot. They sat there for about five minutes before a new Ford Explorer pulled in beside them, with Moose at the wheel.

Noah and Sarah got out as Moose did, and met him in front of the blue car. "How long before anyone knows it's missing?" Noah asked.

"Several hours, at least. I didn't exactly steal it; my alter ego, Jimmy McCormick, is taking it for an extended test drive. I convinced the salesman I needed to take it down to Jefferson City to show my mother, told him I was thinking of buying it as a present for her. Had to leave a five-hundred-dollar deposit, but I didn't think you'd mind. The only thing I did was switch out the dealer plates for the ones off the van. The dealer tag is in the trunk."

Noah nodded, his eyes wide. "Good thinking," he said. "If everything goes well, we can switch back again later and you can turn it back in without a problem."

Moose grinned and looked at Sarah. "It's not as fast as the Chrysler, but it did pretty good on the way here. I was kinda surprised, that thing really handles pretty well."

They traded keys and Sarah slid behind the wheel of the newer car, while Noah got in on the passenger side. As they backed out, they noticed Moose walking into the McDonald's, and Sarah waved at him.

The Ford had a full tank of gas, so they began to just cruise around town. They drove through a couple of the local parks, cruised around the University and finally parked at a small shopping center not far from Alejandra Gomez's home. Noah had called Neil a couple of times, but the boy said there had been no sign of the nanny or children.

At just past noon, however, the situation changed. Noah's phone rang and he snatched it up instantly. "Go!"

"Boss, I'm not a hundred percent sure if this is what you want, but it may be the best you're going to get. Mrs. Gomez and the nanny just loaded the kids into a car and they're pulling away from the house right now. I've hacked into the traffic cams all around the area, give me a couple of minutes and I'll tell you which direction they're going."

"Good, let's go for it. If I have to, I'll take out Alejandra now. Between that and the kids disappearing, we'll probably still get the prayer meeting we want." He motioned for Sarah to start the car and pointed in the general direction of the Gomez house. She pulled out of the parking lot onto the street, and began moving, keeping below the speed limit until she knew which direction to go.

"Okay, she just turned off of North Glenwood onto West Broadway, heading west. Where you at?"

"We're at West Boulevard and Broadway, so she's coming right at us. What's she driving?"

"An SUV, a Lexus. Looks like a new one, it's black."

Noah was nodding his head. "Okay, good, we'll pick her up. Good job, Neil."

"You guys just be careful, okay, Boss? Remember, I have absolutely no interest in working with any other team but Camelot. Don't you go getting yourself killed."

Noah promised to try to obey, and ended the call. Less than a minute later, they spotted the Lexus coming toward them, so Sarah pulled into a parking lot on the right. She cruised through it slowly as the Lexus went by, then pulled out behind it with only a couple of cars in between.

"Don't lose her," Noah said. "We need a spot where I can make my move, so just hang back a bit until you see them park."

"I know," Sarah said. "Don't worry, Babe, this is why they pay me the big bucks."

She kept the Lexus in sight as they cruised across a good part of the city, and then it turned right on a red light onto Stadium Boulevard. Sarah got hung up at the light for a few seconds, but managed to make the turn without losing sight of the Lexus and was only a couple of cars behind when it turned in to the Columbia Mall.

"Oh-oh," Sarah said, "this may not be good."

"Just keep her in sight," Noah replied. "Let's see what's going on here."

The Lexus made its way directly to the Dillard's entrance and stopped, while Sarah hung back in one of the aisles. The passenger side front door opened and the nanny stepped out, then went to the rear of the vehicle and opened the tailgate. She took out and unfolded a double stroller, closed the tailgate and went back to the passenger side. A moment later she had removed both children from the car and put them into the stroller. Noah and Sarah could just see Mrs. Gomez wave as she drove away.

"Get up there, now," Noah said, and Sarah pushed the SUV quickly. The nanny was bustling about, buckling the children into the stroller, when they pulled up beside her. Noah stepped out right beside the nanny, who looked up at him and smiled.

The smile vanished a second later when she saw the pistol he flashed from under his shirt. "Get the kids and get into the car, right now," he said. "You won't be harmed if you do exactly what I say."

The woman looked to be in her late teens or very early 20s, and it was obvious that she was about to panic. Noah reached down and picked up the baby girl. "Get the other child and get into the car," he said. "Please do not make me tell you again."

The girl swallowed, but she undid the buckle she had just fastened on the little boy and slid obediently into the backseat with him. Noah passed the baby in to her and shut the door. Sarah turned in the seat and kept the nanny covered with her own nine-millimeter Beretta while Noah opened the rear hatch, quickly folded down the stroller and put it inside, along with the big diaper bag the nanny had been carrying. He got back into the front seat and Sarah slipped her gun back into her purse as she drove calmly away.

Noah leaned over the seat and took the nanny's purse, scanned through it briefly and found her cell phone. There were no other electronic devices in the purse, so he passed it back to her.

"Please, Señor," the girl said, with tears beginning to fall from her eyes. "Please, please do not hurt the children."

"I have no intention of harming the children or you," Noah said to her. "It's simply necessary for me to remove the children from the situation they're in. You will be with us for a little while and then you will be released. You have my word on it."

"But, Señor, you do not understand," the girl said, her eyes wide. "These children, they belong to some very powerful people, very bad people. If you let me go, they will kill me because this has happened."

Noah looked over the back of the seat at her. "I can promise you that won't happen," he said. "Please be quiet until we get where we're going. As I said, you won't be harmed and we'll do everything we can to make sure you're comfortable as long as you're with us."

He looked around the area as Sarah pulled out onto Stadium Boulevard again, but no one seemed to be paying any attention. He took out his phone and dialed Neil, who answered instantly.

"Phase Two is in hand," Noah said. "Try to get into the security video system at Columbia Mall, especially in front of the Dillard's store. I'm sure they got us on video as I made the snatch, so I'm counting on you to wipe it out. Tell Moose we need to trade cars again, and to meet us out at the East Broadway entrance to Stephens Lake Park."

SIX

Sarah turned left on Broadway, and followed it across the city until she got to the park. The warehouse was actually closer to the park than they had been, so Moose was already waiting with the Chrysler. There were no other cars close by, and Noah had already scouted the area to be sure there were no security cameras. They transferred the nanny and children into the silver car, and Noah remembered to grab the stroller and diaper bag. Sarah drove away while Moose was switching the license plates back.

It was only about a ten-minute ride to the warehouse, and Noah called ahead to tell Neil to open the overhead door. They pulled the car right inside and stayed in it until the overhead door was closed again.

Noah got out and retrieved the stroller, then opened the driver side rear door. He reached in and took the little boy and put him in the stroller, while the nanny brought out the girl.

"This young lady," he said, indicating Sarah, "will show you where you will be staying for right now. Some people will be coming to pick you up and take you somewhere else before long, but until then just let us know if there's anything you need." He handed her the diaper bag and walked alongside as she followed Sarah to the room that had been prepared for them.

Sarah showed her the refrigerator with soft drinks and snacks, then gave her the remote for the little television they had set up. "If you need anything, knock on the door. Someone will be here all the time, you won't be left alone."

"Please, please, you don't understand," the girl said. "The children, their mother and father, they will kill me."

Sarah shook her head sadly. "They won't," she said. "I can guarantee you, they won't." She pulled the door shut behind herself and slid the heavy-duty locking bolt home, then added the padlock they had installed for extra security.

She walked over to where Noah and Neil were sitting by the computer and dropped into a chair. Noah was on the phone, speaking with Allison. He nodded into the phone and then ended the call.

"Neil wiped out the security footage at the mall," he said, "so we should be in the clear on that. Our people will be here for the girl and the kids in about four hours. Queen Allison is sending them in one of the jets. She wants those kids out of Missouri as soon as possible, and so do I."

Sarah nodded. "Okay, so now what? We just wait?"

Noah picked up the nanny's cell phone from the table in front of him. "I don't think we want to wait," he said. The phone was an older one, and it took him only a few moments to find Alejandra Gomez in the contact list. He handed the phone to Neil.

Neil plugged a cord into its hands-free jack, tapped a few keys on the computer and then pushed the button to make the call. It was answered only seconds later.

"Si, Margarita?" he heard.

A voice emanated from the computer as Neil spoke into a microphone. "Mrs. Gomez," he said in Spanish, "since I know you recognize this number, you'll understand that what I'm telling you is the truth. I have your children. They will be returned to you in exchange for ten million dollars. I will call you later tonight with instructions on where to bring the money."

He cut off the call even as Mrs. Gomez was demanding to speak to the nanny, and then Noah took the phone and smashed it on the concrete floor. When he was certain that it was broken, he tossed the pieces into a metal barrel that had a thin layer of oil in the bottom, then balled up some paper and lit it with a lighter from his pocket. When he tossed it into the barrel, there was a *whoosh* as the oil caught fire. It burned for only a couple of minutes, and Noah opened a nearby window to let the smoke out.

"What did you think?" Neil said. "I probably rehearsed that at least a hundred times, you know."

"It was fine," Noah said. He sat down beside the kid and reached over to turn on the scanner. Moose walked in a moment later and joined them as they waited.

"Everything go okay, turning the car back in?" Noah asked.

Moose grinned. "Went fine, except I think I got a salesman all pissed off at me. I told him Mom didn't like the car, so she was going with a Chevy instead."

"Yeah, that ought to do it," Neil said. "Just hope he doesn't get in trouble for letting you take it out for so long."

"He shouldn't, not as long as they don't figure out it was used in a kidnapping."

"Hopefully no one will catch on to that," Noah said. "The car had different tags on it, and any security video footage from the mall got erased by Mr. Wizard, here. I sincerely doubt anyone will connect that car to what happened, which means they won't connect back to Jimmy McCormick, either."

"So, now we just wait?" Moose asked.

"Yep," Noah said. "Neil used the nanny's phone to call Alejandra Gomez, so she's probably already sounded the alarm. That was a good ten minutes ago, and there's nothing on the police scanner yet. I have my doubts they'll even be called in, at least not yet. These people like to handle things on their own."

"You should have given me Old Lady Gomez's phone number," Neil said. "I could have hacked it so we could listen in to her phone calls. I was going to suggest it, but you smashed the phone too fast."

Noah shrugged. "Just keep watching the cameras at her house, I'm pretty sure we'll know when things hit the fan."

An hour passed by, and Neil reported seeing a few cars coming and going from the Gomez place. Mrs. Gomez's Lexus had returned, so the visitors were probably friends and associates who had heard about the children's abduction. Noah nodded. "Let's go ahead and order some flowers from the other shops in town. Do it in Spanish, so that it sounds like it's coming from some of their own people." He turned to Moose. "I think it's safe for you to go ahead and take some flowers over there. If they seem surprised, just shrug like you don't know anything."

Moose nodded. "Hey, all I know is I get paid to drive the truck. They tell me where to deliver flowers, and I go do it. What do I do if they want the office number?"

"Good question," Noah said. "Give them Sarah's phone number. She can pretend to be the receptionist if they call."

"You got it," Moose said, and then he got up and left.

Neil watched as first Moose, and then two other delivery vans delivered flowers to the Gomez household. The occasional vehicle was still stopping at the house, but didn't stay very long. It was just over an hour later when he reported that cars began converging on the Gomez house and staying there.

"Sounds like it's about to begin, then," Noah said. "Neil, get into the security company's video server and make sure there's no trace of Moose making any deliveries there. Cops and feds are going to be all over that footage in just a little while, we don't want anything tying us to it."

He rose from his chair and looked at Sarah.

"That's our cue," he said, and she got up without a word to follow him to the car. Moose went to open the overhead door, and Sarah backed out and turned onto the street. She began making her way toward the house while Noah pulled out his phone and got Neil on the line.

"It'll take us about fifteen or twenty minutes to get there," he said. "I'm going to keep you on the line and on speaker, so give me a running count on targets."

"Will do," Neil said. "It looks like Mr. and Mrs. Perez and their daughters, and the entire Hernandez clan have arrived. Wait, there's another car pulling up now—it's Menendez, with all of his sons. There's a lot of people there, already, at least twenty or more. Hold on—okay, there's Armando Rodriguez and his bunch. Boss, you got the whole kit and caboodle in there right now. Oh, shit, wait a minute—there's a couple of people that aren't on our list. What about them, Boss?"

"We try to minimize collateral damage, Neil, but it's a safe bet that anyone associating with these people is somehow involved in the things they do. If you start seeing more who aren't on the list than the ones who are, I might have to rethink this."

"Damn. No, it's just a couple people, so far. Everybody else that I see is part of one of the families."

"They're moving pretty fast, then," Noah said. "Keep me posted. If anyone leaves, let me know immediately." He looked over at Sarah. "Get us there as fast as you can," he said.

Sarah grinned, and the car launched itself forward. Within seconds she was doing more than sixty miles an hour down the narrow street, and narrowly missed crashing into a car that backed unexpectedly out of a driveway. She had two wheels up on the curb, but managed to get around it without hitting anything.

It took eight minutes to get to the street where the gathering was taking place, and Noah had her cruise past the house once. More than a dozen cars were in the driveway and lined up along the street, so Noah told her to go to the next intersection and turn around, then stop the car.

She did as he instructed her, and Noah noticed that she was breathing heavily as he pulled the detonator remote out of his shirt pocket. He pressed the button for channel 7, looked straight ahead at the house and dropped his thumb onto the trigger button.

The house disintegrated. A ball of flame suddenly came into existence, and a moment later there was a fair-sized mushroom cloud over where it had stood. Debris flew in every direction, and even though the neighboring houses were some distance away, many of their windows shattered instantly. There was considerable heat damage to their exteriors, but the most extensive devastation went straight upward with the heat of the explosion.

"Oh, my God," Sarah breathed. She sat there staring, her eyes wide, as the fireball rose into the sky. "That almost looked like a nuclear blast," she said.

Cars had been thrown around in front of the house like plastic models, and alarms were sounding all over the place. People from surrounding houses were hurrying out to look in the direction of the explosion. Noah reached over and touched Sarah's shoulder.

"Time to go," he said.

Sarah turned her face to look at him, her eyes still wide, and he saw tears streaming down her face. She nodded once, then put the car in reverse and took her foot off the brake. She backed around the corner, and then turned to go in the opposite direction from the remains of the house.

Before they had gone half a mile, police cars and fire engines were streaming toward the explosion. Sarah drove sedately, carefully avoiding drawing any attention to them as she maneuvered through the streets. Whenever an emergency vehicle appeared on the road, she pulled over to the side and waited for it to pass, then changed the color of the car as soon as she could do so without being observed.

Because of such delays, it took almost three-quarters of an hour for them to get back to the warehouse, and they left the car outside. They walked in and joined Moose and Neil, who were listening to the police scanner as it spewed forth voices. The explosion had jarred the city, and all of the emergency services were scrambling to try to figure out what to do.

"First responders said they found body parts all over the neighborhood," Moose said. "They're already claiming a death toll of more than twenty-five, but I think they're just guessing based on the number of arms and legs. This little city's never seen anything like this."

"I know I never saw anything like that before," Sarah said. "My God, I couldn't believe it. That whole house just suddenly disappeared, and then there was this giant fireball. It looked like the old movies you see of nuclear bombs going off."

Neil turned around in his chair and looked at her. "Sarah? Are you okay?"

She looked at him for a moment, then nodded her head slowly. "Yeah, I'll be all right," she said. "I mean, I knew what we were here to do, I just—I never expected it to look like that. It was—I'd have to say it was one of the most incredible things I've ever seen, but it was also one of the most terrible."

Moose laid a hand on her shoulder. "Well, at least you can be pretty sure nobody inside suffered. Getting blown to bits is pretty much an instantaneous way to die."

Sarah turned her head to face him. "Didn't suffer? Those people have been responsible for how many thousands and thousands of deaths? Do you think I care if they suffered? I'm just sort of in shock, I guess, because I never expected to see anything like that." She looked at Noah, and then at Neil. "Look, guys, I knew what I was getting into when I agreed to join E & E, I know what we do. I'm not upset about the people who died in the house, I'm just shocked at seeing it completely obliterated like that."

There was a sudden banging on the door to the room where the nanny and children were waiting, and they heard the girl screaming something in Spanish. Noah got up and went to the door, unlocked it and slowly pulled it open.

The girl was standing there, her face ashen. "The TV, Señor, they say there was an explosion. On the news, they show the helicopter, it is flying over the fire. Señor, it was the house of my employers, no?"

Noah nodded slowly. "Yes, it was," he said. "You don't have to worry about them doing anything to you. They're gone."

She turned and looked over her shoulder at where the two children were laying in their cribs. "But, Señor, this is their babies. What will I do, what will I do with them?"

"They'll be going to a new home. You'll be going with them for a little while, and then you'll be allowed to return to your home."

She spun to face him again. "My home? I will go home?"

Noah nodded. "Yes, you'll go home. You will go and talk with some people first, maybe for a few days, but then you will get to go home."

The girl stood there and stared at him for a moment, then slowly nodded her own head. She turned around and walked over to the bed and sat down on it, and Noah closed the door. He bolted it, but did not use the padlock.

"I actually think she was relieved," he said as he sat down again. "I don't know if she was involved in the drug business at all, but she didn't seem all that upset about Mr. and Mrs. Gomez being gone."

They sat and listened to the scanner for another couple of hours, and then Noah's phone rang. He answered it, and quickly gave directions to the warehouse. Twenty minutes later, a car pulled up outside the building and two women walked inside.

One of the women was Hispanic, and was able to explain more fully to the nanny what was going on. They had brought along car seats for the children, and had all three of them loaded up into their car within just a few minutes.

"So, you're Camelot?" The woman who asked shook her head. "From everything I've heard about you, I thought you'd be a lot bigger, with fireballs shooting out of your ass. Don't worry about these kids, they'll be well taken care of. A week from now, they'll be in a new home with loving parents. We've already got them picked out."

She turned and joined her partner in the car, and they drove away.

SEVEN

"Let's pack it up," Noah said. "I want everything we need to take with us in the trunk of the car, ready to go at a moment's notice. Everything else goes into the van. Sarah, you and Neil start packing the flowers into the van. Moose and I will start taking down the furniture in the guestroom. Everything goes in the van, we don't leave anything behind."

"What about the 3-D printer?" Neil asked. "Shouldn't it go in the van? It takes up a lot of room."

Noah shook his head. "No, I want it in the car; don't worry, the trunk is big, it'll fit. I just don't want to leave any traces behind that can link us to the Gomez explosion, and people may have seen the van when Moose dropped off the shrine. We're taking it out of the city, someplace isolated, and then I'm going to detonate all those flowerpots. That'll get rid of the van and everything we bought while we were here, and cause more confusion while we beat it out of town."

It took them less than an hour to get everything loaded. Neil had gone online and found a likely spot for ditching the van, so Moose took the van and headed for it by one route while Noah, Sarah and Neil took the car and went by another.

There were police cars just about everywhere, including city police, sheriff's deputies and state police. They were cruising the streets, obviously looking for anything that looked out of place. According to the scanner, a ten-block area around the explosion had been sealed off, but the rest of the city was still open. The massive police presence was simply precautionary, but it looked like everyone was driving as carefully as they could.

Neil had chosen an abandoned rock quarry that sat about eight miles north of the city. They found it with no trouble, and Moose was there waiting for them in the van.

The quarry wasn't very big, but it was deep. The big square pit in the center went down over two hundred feet, with a roadway that spiraled around its walls. The whole property was surrounded by a chain-link fence, but Moose had already picked the lock by the time Noah, Sarah and Neil arrived. They drove carefully down to the bottom, where Moose climbed into the back seat of the sedan beside Neil.

"Good thing this car has all-wheel drive," Moose said. "I don't think the van would've made it back up out of this hole."

"It doesn't have to," Noah said. "As soon as we get up out of here, I'm blowing it up."

He actually waited until they had pulled out of the gate and locked it before he set off the explosives in the van. It was down deep enough in the hole that the sound was muffled, but the fireball that rose up from the pit in the ground was even bigger than the one that had leveled the Gomez house. They sat in the car and watched it for a moment, then Sarah turned her eyes to the road and began driving back into the city by a winding, circuitous route.

They made a quick stop at a KFC to pick up a bucket of chicken for dinner, so it was nearly nine o'clock by the time they got back to their hotel. Noah was not surprised to see a deputy sheriff standing at the front desk. Checking to see who was registered in local hotels and motels would be a logical part of police procedure after such an explosion, and the deputy turned and looked at them as they entered.

Noah took Sarah's hand and went into his "normal guy" mode as he walked quickly toward the officer.

"Hey, there," he said, his face looking slightly worried. "Is something wrong? We heard about the bombing, is that terrorists? Are we in danger here at the hotel?"

His nervous chatter put the deputy at ease, and he smiled. "I don't think it was terrorists," he said. "We just like to get an idea of who was in town when something like this happens, it's just routine. I don't think you've got anything to worry about, the FBI seems to think the explosion might have been related to some drug gangs in the area."

Noah's jaw dropped, and his eyes went wide. "Drug gangs? Holy shit, you mean drug gangs are using bombs nowadays? Man, this world's gone crazy, hasn't it?"

The deputy nodded, still smiling but obviously becoming impatient to get on with his business. "Yeah, it sure has," he said. "Well, Sir, you have a good night, okay? I've got to get back to work."

"Oh, yeah, I'm sorry," Noah said. Sarah tugged on his hand and said, "Come on, Baby, I'm tired." Noah smiled once more at the deputy, then turned and walked with her toward the elevator. Moose and Neil had gone up ahead of them carrying the food, and they found them waiting in the hall outside their rooms.

Once again, they all went into Noah and Sarah's room and sat down to eat. Sarah turned on the TV; news of the explosion and investigation was dominating all of the local channels and some of the national ones.

The FBI had made it into town, as the deputy had said, and one of their spokesmen told a number of reporters that they were looking at the possibility of a drug-related hit. There was no word yet on what type of explosives might have been used, but the devastation seemed to indicate that it was definitely something powerful. The spokesman said that the FBI was working with local and state authorities, and was actively looking for several suspects.

The television displayed two pictures, photos of men who were considered to be suspects in the bombing. Ironically, they were photographs of Armando Rodriguez and Carlos Perez. According to the spokesman, they were known associates of Enrique and Alejandra Gomez, and there had been rumors of a rivalry in their organization over the past few months.

"Good luck finding either one of them," Neil said around a chicken leg. "You'd have to sweep up a lot of debris and go through it for DNA to find those guys."

"Nah," Moose said, "they can probably find a finger or two, get prints off of those."

Sarah looked at the two of them. "I don't think either one of you guys has ever grown up," she said. "You're like twelve-year-olds, you think anything gross or disgusting is funny."

Both men looked at her in silence for a moment, and then Neil grinned. "Gee, thanks, Sarah," he said. "I think that's the nicest compliment you've ever given us." He went back to chomping on the chicken leg.

Noah had watched the exchange, but just shook his head. "We'll be leaving in the morning," he said. "I don't think it will be any surprise when people start checking out of hotels around town after this, so let's be ready to get up early and head out. I'm sure I'll hear from Allison in the morning, but domestic mission protocol says we don't call in for at least twenty-four hours after completion, in case the authorities are monitoring phone calls."

Neil dropped the leg bone into the now-empty bucket. "No problem," he said, "I'm ready to get some sleep, anyway."

"Yeah, me too," Moose echoed. "What time you want us up and ready in the morning?"

"I want to look normal. We'll check out around seven thirty, then maybe hit Denny's again for breakfast before we get on the road."

The guys agreed, and left the room. Sarah finished the last bite of her chicken and headed for the shower. She paused at the bathroom doorway and looked back at Noah.

"You coming?"

* * * * *

The team checked out on schedule and was back on the road by eight thirty that morning. They had put more than fifty miles behind them by the time Noah's cell phone rang at just after nine.

"Good morning, Camelot," he heard Allison say. "From all the reports, it appears you have had a successful mission."

"It seemed to come out okay," Noah said. "We managed to get them all together in one place, and take the whole lot of them out at once."

"Yes, and I can't wait for the debriefing on this one. Our friends at DEA are freaking out a bit, they didn't expect you to make such a big hole in the city. I told them they got what they ordered and to shut up. Of course, that doesn't stop the FBI from running their mouths, but nothing ever does."

"Well, I hope I haven't caused you any problems," Noah said. "You told me to make a statement, and I think I did."

Allison burst out laughing. "Let me tell you something, Camelot," she said. "I've been up since four o'clock this morning, getting calls from every agency chief you can imagine. You have shaken not only the Angelos Cartel, but every drug cartel in Latin America. From what I'm hearing, they're having trouble getting anyone to think about coming in and taking over. As for the feds, they're in heaven. Your explosion, because it looks like all of your targets were eliminated, gave them everything they needed to get warrants to search the remaining homes. They're finding all kinds of stuff, even evidence of dirty cops in the area. They'll be having a field day for at least six months out of this."

"Glad to hear it. We should be home late tonight. You want us in tomorrow morning for debrief?"

"Absolutely," Allison said. "I'll have the coffee and doughnuts ready. Great job, Camelot, tell your team for me."

Noah put the phone away. "Queen Allison says we did a good job," he said. "I guess it gave the DEA an excuse to get warrants on the rest of the targets, and they're having a lot of fun with it."

"We debrief in the morning?" Moose asked.

"Yep. Bright and early, of course. Breakfast in the conference room, coffee and doughnuts."

Neil groaned. "Is there something in the operations manual that says we aren't allowed to get enough sleep? Why couldn't we debrief at noon? Lunch, instead of breakfast?"

They rode along, occasionally engaging in further banter. Noah joined in sometimes, but mostly he was quiet.

Noah had always enjoyed watching scenery pass by, and this day was no exception. There were some beautiful forested areas in the western half of Missouri, places he'd enjoy visiting sometime.

When they got into Kansas, however, the scenery began to flatten out. Before long, Noah had to admit to himself that it was boring, until he finally just leaned his head back and went to sleep.

He woke a couple of hours later, as Sarah pulled off the interstate to get gas. When she parked at the pumps, he got out and pumped the gas himself, using the opportunity to stretch his legs. Neil and Moose went inside the station in search of snacks and soft drinks, while Sarah stood beside Noah.

She glanced at the engagement ring on her finger. "I'm gonna hate giving this back," she said. "I know it's just a fantasy, but it's been kind of a nice one."

Noah looked at her. "I don't know that getting married would be a good idea for us," he said. "I'm still waiting for you to get tired of me. Everybody else always has."

She looked at him, her expression slightly angry. "In case you haven't noticed, I'm not everybody else."

He shrugged. "No, you're certainly not," he said. "On the other hand, you said what attracted you to me was the fact that there wouldn't be any strings attached. Getting married would probably be more like a rope, don't you think?"

"I didn't say I wanted to get married," Sarah said bitterly. "I said it was a nice fantasy. You know what fantasy is? It's something you daydream about, even though you know it isn't going to happen."

"Why would you daydream about it if you don't believe it can happen? That doesn't make any sense."

Sarah stared at him for a moment, and then turned her face away from him. "Just when I think you're starting to get it," she mumbled.

The gas pump cut off as the tank reached full, Moose and Neil came back out with chips, beef jerky and bottles of soda pop, and they got back on the road. The two in the back looked at Sarah's hands, white-knuckling the wheel, and then glanced at each other. Neil shrugged, and Moose just shook his head.

The scenery stayed just as boring as before, so Noah leaned his head back again. He was just about to doze off when his cell phone went off again, signaling a text message. All three of the others suddenly grabbed their phones, as each of them had received a text at the same time.

Neverland under attack. Go to ground until further.

Sarah looked at Noah, her face in shock. "They're under attack?"

Noah shook his head. "You know everything I do. Protocol says we duck low and stay there, so let's find somewhere to hole up."

"Boss, what?" Moose asked. "Shouldn't we get back and try to help?"

"You read the policy manual, same as I did. In the event Neverland is compromised, all field agents are to stop whatever they're doing and find somewhere to lay low. They'll contact us when it's safe to come in."

"Holy geez," Neil said. "What about Lacey, I need to call her. Moose, what about Elaine?"

"No calls," Noah said, "not right now. We don't know what's going on back there, and any phone calls into the complex could end up causing problems. If we haven't heard anything by tonight, you can call and check in with them, but you'll do it on burner phones. If they're compromised, we don't need to leave a trail back to us."

"But, Noah…" Neil began, before Noah cut him off.

"No calls, that's the protocol. Like I said, if we haven't heard anything by tonight, we'll get some throwaway phones and you can call both of them. For right now, we do things by the book."

Neil started to argue, but knew he wouldn't get anywhere. He flopped back in the seat and turned his face to look out the window, but not before Sarah saw the tears trying to brim over from his eyes.

She glanced at Noah. "He's scared," she whispered. "I think Lacey is his first girlfriend, he's worried about her."

"I understand that," Noah said just as softly. "We still have to follow protocol. I'll bend it for them later this evening, but for right now we're staying by the book."

EIGHT

"We need a motel," Noah said, "someplace inconspicuous and out-of-the-way. Neil, see what you can find."

Neil groaned as he picked up his computer from where it sat between him and Moose and opened it up. With its built-in broadband system, he had access to the internet from almost anywhere on earth. It took him only a few moments to locate a motel that would suit their purposes.

"Two exits up," he said listlessly, "there's a place called the Wagon Trail Motel. It's about two miles off the interstate, to the south. Looks about as inconspicuous as you can get."

"That'll do," Noah said. Sarah nodded, and took the second exit when they got to it.

The Wagon Trail Motel looked like it had seen better days, but it would suit their purposes nicely. Rather than being a single building with a lot of rooms, there were numerous cabins scattered around a five-acre lot. Noah went into the office and rented two of them, telling the desk clerk that they were interested in buying some property in the area and might want to stay a day or two.

Their cabins were side-by-side, and they carried their bags into them before gathering in the one that Noah and Sarah would occupy. Unlike a normal motel room, the cabins included a small kitchen. Noah commented that if they had to stay a few days, at least they wouldn't have to keep putting up with restaurant food.

They sat and talked for a little while, trying to guess what kind of attack might have taken Neverland by surprise, but they simply didn't have any information to go on. Neil continued to whine about wanting to call Lacey, but Noah wouldn't budge on the matter. They finally decided the only smart thing to do was get some rest while they could, so Neil and Moose went back to their own cabin.

Noah and Sarah lay on the bed, and he kept an arm wrapped around her as she snuggled up to him. They talked for a few moments, but then Noah drifted off to sleep. Sarah lay and watched them for a while, envious for the moment of his ability to shut out everything else when he needed to sleep.

When he awoke two hours later, Noah found Sarah still awake and watching. She smiled and crinkled her eyes when he looked at her, then pulled his face down for a kiss.

"That seems like a nice way to wake up," he said. "Did you sleep at all?"

She shook her head. "Hmm-mm. Just been laying here watching you. I didn't know how long you wanted to sleep, so I just laid here."

Noah picked up his phone from the nightstand beside him and glanced at it. It was nearly one thirty in the afternoon, but there were no text messages or missed calls. "I guess it's time I got up. I was hoping we would have heard something by now."

"Me, too," Sarah said. "Could I make a suggestion?"

"Sure, Babe," Noah said. "What is it?"

"Let Neil and Moose call the girls. Assuming they're okay, both of their dads work for the head office. They probably know something."

Noah lay there and looked at her for a moment, then nodded. "I think you got a good point, but we need some throwaway phones. There was a sign on the road out front for a McDonald's a few miles ahead. If the town is big enough for that, there's probably a Walmart. Why don't you run on in and get some burner phones, and maybe pick up something for dinner."

"Okay," Sarah said. She kissed him on the end of his nose as she rolled off the bed and slipped into her shoes again, picked up her purse and slipped out the door. Noah heard the car start a moment later, and she drove away.

He thumbed the speed dial icon for Moose and put the phone to his ear.

"You guys awake? Okay, then get over here. I just sent Sarah to get some burner phones. It's time we find out what's going on, if we can." He ended the call without saying goodbye, and there was a tap on the door only a minute later. "Come on in."

Moose and Neil stepped inside and sat down in chairs at the small table. Noah got up from the bed and went to join them.

"I haven't heard anything, so I'm sure neither of you have, either. Sarah is going to pick up something for dinner while she's out, too. Soon as she gets back, you guys can make your calls."

"Damn, I wish she'd hurry," Neil said. "If anything has happened to Lacey, I'll go nuts."

"Lacey's a smart girl," Moose said, "and her daddy is one of the toughest men I've ever known. I think she'll be okay. Elaine, too."

The three of them sat and talked for another half hour, until Sarah returned. She stepped inside with three bags, and handed one of them to Neil immediately. The skinny kid ripped it open to find two prepaid disposable phones. He passed one to Moose and then began ripping at the package on the other. It took them only a couple of minutes to have the phones assembled and activated.

"Neil," Noah said when Neil looked at him, "go ahead and call Lacey. Make sure she's okay, and then see if she knows anything about what's going on."

Neil's eyes lit up as his thumb flew over the dial pad and put the phone on speaker. They heard the one on the other end ring four times, and Neil was starting to panic when Lacey finally answered.

"Hello," she said cautiously.

Neil gasped in relief. "Hey, honey, it's me! Are you okay?"

"Yeah, I'm all right," she said. "Do you know what's going on?"

"No, honey, we don't. I was calling to see if you might know something."

"I don't know a lot," Lacey said. "I know somebody walked into the offices and just started blasting away. I heard there were seven dead, one of them was Jenny Atkins, the Dragon Lady's secretary. Ms. Peterson and Mr. Jefferson were both wounded, but I don't know how bad it is. They're in the hospital, but nobody is saying much of anything about it."

"Allison was wounded?" Noah asked suddenly. "Who's in command?"

"I'm not sure, at the moment," Lacey said. "I haven't heard anything more since it happened a few hours ago. I tried calling my dad, but he hasn't gotten back to me yet. He was supposed to go to the office sometime today, but I don't know if he was there when the attack happened or not. Oh, Neil, I'm so worried."

Noah glanced at Moose, who was holding his own burner phone in his hand. He nodded once, and Moose got up and walked outside, dialing Elaine's phone number.

"Lacey, where are you?" Neil asked. "Are you at home?"

"Yeah," she said. "I was off today, mom and I were going to go do some shopping this afternoon, but when this happened we decided to just stay home and wait."

Noah leaned forward. "Lacey, is anything on the news about this?"

"Yes, but they're just calling it a random attack at the moment. The Kirtland police are actually some of our people, but they have to stay in their characters. The FBI is here, doing whatever they do. That's all I really know right now."

Noah nodded, and Neil took the phone off speaker. He moved to the other side of the room so that he could have some privacy, and Noah turned to Sarah.

"Noah, who could have done this?" Sarah asked. "I mean, you don't think it was…"

"We don't know enough to even make a guess," Noah said, "but I wouldn't put it past Nicolaich. We know he's out there, operating on his own now. I'd have to say it's possible he blames E & E, and me personally, for his little regime falling apart. He's probably the only one I could imagine right now who would have the balls to make an attack like this, but we just don't know enough to even really speculate."

Moose stepped back inside, the phone to his ear. "Noah, Donald Jefferson is in critical condition at Kirtland Regional. Elaine says they don't know right now if he's going to make it at all. Allison Peterson was taken by life flight to Denver, nobody knows anything since then. Her secretary was killed in the attack, along with six other people. Doc Parker is in temporary command, but that's just because they can't find John Hackett. John is actually the number three, after Allison and Donald."

Noah nodded. "Tell her we appreciate it, and we hope the best for her father." He took out his cell phone and dialed the number to Allison's office.

"Brigadoon Investments," answered a voice he didn't recognize. "How may I direct your call?"

"Doc Parker, please," Noah said.

"And may I ask who's calling?"

"Yes, tell him it's Noah Wolf."

The operator placed him on hold, but he was only there for a moment. Doc Parker's voice came on the line after only a few seconds.

"What was the first thing I ever told you?" Parker asked, his voice gruff and challenging.

Noah thought for only a second, then said, "You told me I was late, and when I said I was new, you told me that didn't matter."

"Very good," Parker said. "Are you on a secure line?"

"Yes, sir, an agency phone. I realize I'm breaking protocol but I'm hearing that we've had some losses up at the top. Is there anything I can do?"

"Well, for right now, you can stay out of here. I'm not going to ream you for checking in, I wasn't going to wait much longer before I called you myself. I've got three teams down right now, and all the others are in the field and can't be reached. You're the only one I've got available right now. We're trying to figure out exactly what hit us, and then I need you to get on it."

"Yes, sir," Noah said. "You said three teams are down?"

"Oz and Unicorn are down for good, dead. Aladdin is alive, but he'll be out of the field for a while, may not ever go back out. Cinderella, Robin Hood and Hercules are out on missions out of the country. That leaves me you. I want you to stay low until I, or someone who replaces me, gives you the word to move. Wait a minute, belay that. I want you to stay low until you have a target to go after, whether you get it from us or find it on your own."

"Yes, sir. Sir, do you know if this has anything to do with Andropov?"

"Oh, yes, he was your problem, wasn't he? We're actually thinking he may be involved, but we don't know if he's running the operation or not. We got hit in four places at once this morning, including this office, the Armory, R&D and the training classrooms. Those three attacks happened first and seemed to be distractions, trying to keep us from being ready for the big one that hit here. We've got a total of eighteen dead, more than fifty wounded, including some of the newest recruits. Don Jefferson was carried out of here with two bullets in his left lung and one in his head, but he was still screaming for a gun as they put him in the ambulance. I always said he was too damned stubborn to kill, and now I'm hoping I was right. Allison, she's in surgery in Denver. She was hit three times, as well, but she got the son of a bitch that shot her. No word yet on her condition. Just found out a few minutes ago that John Hackett bought the farm, so I guess I'm stuck with this job for a while. I've got Art Jackson subbing for Jefferson."

"I can't think of anybody better than you, right now, sir," Noah said. "Would you let me know about Allison when you hear something? Other than that, I will await your orders."

"I'll do that," Parker said. "Meanwhile, you got that bright boy, the skinny kid, what's his name? Blessing, that's it, Blessing. Put his ass to work, see if he can find anything on Andropov. And if you can track the bastard down, you are authorized to take him out. That also applies to any of his associates that might be involved."

"Yes, sir," Noah said. "We'll get on it right now."

Noah looked over to where Neil was still talking to Lacey on his phone, and hooked a finger at him. Neil told Lacey he would call her back later and sat down across from Noah again. Moose had gone back outside after delivering his report, but he stepped in just a moment later and took his own chair.

"They've got Allison in surgery," Noah said, "but we don't know anything yet. Jefferson's in the hospital in Kirtland, apparently he took a couple in the chest and a hit in the head, but Doc Parker says he was still conscious when they carried him out. That could be a good sign. They found John Hackett, but he's dead, so Parker is in charge for now. Mr. Jackson is acting as his deputy." He turned to Neil. "I need you to get online, see what you can find out about Nicolaich Andropov. I don't know the details, but Doc Parker seems to think that he was involved in this attack, and if he was, then I want to find him as soon as we can. We are authorized to act on our own and go after him."

Neil jumped up and ran out the door, but came back a few moments later with his computer. He plugged it in and turned it on as Moose turned to Noah.

"What can I do, Boss?" Moose asked.

Noah glanced at Sarah, who was busying herself with the little kitchen, then turned back to Moose. "Right now, I think the most important thing for you to do is try to help me keep things on an even keel. We've got to focus, Moose, try to either come up with a game plan on our own, or sit and wait to see what the home office has to say. Doc Parker didn't seem to know when they might be back up to running properly."

Moose nodded. "Okay. I just want to be able to check in with Elaine, now and then, is that all right?"

"Yeah, at this point I'd have to say it's not a problem. They're putting everything back together as quickly as they can and I'm certain security there is as high as it could possibly be right now."

Neil cleared his throat, and Noah looked at him. "Noah? You said Mr. Jackson is okay?"

"Yes, he's helping Doc Parker run the show for right now, doing Mr. Jefferson's job."

Neil turned and looked at him. "Would you mind if I take a minute and call Lacey back? She and her mom are worried sick, they haven't heard from her dad since the attack started."

Noah looked at him for a moment, then nodded. "Be careful what you say," he said. "You're not on a secure line, so don't give her too many details. Don't mention Doc Parker, just say that you got word that her father is okay."

Neil grinned and nodded, and hit the redial button on his prepaid phone instantly. Noah sat quietly as Neil became a hero to his girlfriend for letting her know that her father was alive and apparently well.

Neil cut the call short and then got back on the computer. He was feeling a rage beginning to build within himself, anger at whoever had done this and caused so much harm and grief. He quietly told himself that it didn't matter who it was, Neil wanted his own chance to take a shot at them.

"Hey, Noah?" Neil asked.

"Yeah?"

"Can you get me a sawed-off shotgun? From everything I've read, even I can hit what I'm shooting at with that."

Noah cocked his head and just looked at the skinny young man for a moment. "Tell you what," he said finally. "I'll see what I can do."

NINE

Sarah had decided on spaghetti, which pleased everyone, and it was done in fairly short order. She scooped it out onto plates and set one in front of each of the three men before making one for herself and taking a seat at the table.

"Be careful, Noah," Moose said. "She's acting domestic. I think that engagement ring must be too tight, it's cutting off circulation to her brain."

Sarah backhanded him on his shoulder. "Shut up, jerk face," she said. "Remember the emergency protocols? We're supposed to remain in character. According to the file they gave me, I'm Rosemary Wingo, engaged to be married sometime soon. Gotta act the part, right?"

Moose chuckled, and Noah simply turned and looked at Sarah. "Realistically, you're right, but if we really were Wyatt and Rosemary, you don't think I'd want you to wait on my friends, do you?"

"You shut up, too," Sarah said as she spun her fork in the spaghetti and shoved it into her mouth.

Neil had spent the time before dinner hacking into every government database he could think of that might have a reference to Nicolaich Andropov. The man had been seen four times over the past two months. He was in Spain first, apparently negotiating an arms deal, then went to Rome for a week. No one seemed to have any idea what he was doing at the time, but then he turned up a couple of weeks later in London, where he was seen entering the North Korean embassy only days before that country escalated its efforts to rekindle the Korean War. He was almost captured there, but managed to slip away from his pursuers at the last second before they were ready to close in.

The most recent sighting of him, though, had been in Los Angeles. He was identified by an FBI agent there on a security video, in the company of an unknown mercenary who was in the process of purchasing weapons. A raid was mounted to try to capture both of them, but it failed.

That was just two weeks previously, but it meant that he was within the United States at least that recently, and that, combined with the fact that he was the only person who might have both the motive and the means to pull off such an operation, was enough to put him at the top of Noah's suspect list for the attack on Neverland. Since that time, however, there had been no news concerning him at all.

"He isn't done," Noah said. "This attack on Neverland, that's just the beginning. Neverland is too big for him to take down, and he knows it. He's not trying that, he's after something specific."

"Yeah," Neil said. "He's after you, Boss. This bastard doesn't ever give up, does he?"

"I'm not sure that makes sense," Noah said. "If he managed to gather enough intel to let them get into our main office, then he probably knows enough about us to figure out who I am. Why would he make an attack like this when I'm not even around? You'd think he'd want to wait until I got home and attack me directly. Why wouldn't he just do that?"

"Because the intel that he had wasn't enough," Neil said. "I'd be willing to bet my Hummer that he was after information, and probably information about you. You pretty much single-handedly destroyed his entire operation. Somehow, I don't think just killing you is enough for him to feel like he's gotten revenge. I think he's out to destroy you, the way you destroyed him. To do that, he's got to find out more about you. He needs to know who you really are, or should I say, who you really were."

Noah's eyebrows lowered as he thought over what Neil had said. "Who I was is dead, with enough high-powered government witnesses to confirm it that he'd never be able to expose me that way. He'd be smart enough to figure that out on his own, so why would he want any more information on me?"

"Background," Sarah said. "Maybe he's trying to find someone in your past that he could use against you."

"I guess that's possible," Noah said. "On the other hand, if he learns anything about me at all, it would probably tell him that such a ploy wouldn't work. I've only been close to two people in my life, before now, but they think I'm dead. Even if he managed to get to them, there'd be nothing I could do for them."

"But that's you," Moose said. "It takes a while to get the idea that you don't operate the way normal people do. Hell, you had to knock the shit out of me before I figured it out. He might try to use some old friend against you, just because he wouldn't know any better."

Noah stared at the wall for a moment, but then shook his head. "No, I think it's something else, but I can't put my finger on it."

"Boss, I think you better think this through again. Remember what happened when he took Sarah? You walked right into the deadliest trap he ever set to get her back. I don't think he understands that you wouldn't do that for everyone."

Noah caught Sarah grinning at him, and she quickly turned away. He picked up his phone and dialed the main office again. A moment later he was talking with Doc Parker once more.

"Sir, we've come up with a theory. Can you tell me if anyone got into our personnel files during the attack?"

"Interesting. We weren't compromised during the attack, no," Parker said. "However, the computer guys say we've been hacked. It probably happened in the last forty-eight hours, and personnel files seemed to be the biggest target."

"Interesting," Noah said. "If the same people were behind the hack, then they already had the information that we thought they might've been after. Well, it was just a theory anyway."

"What was the theory, Camelot?" Doc Parker asked.

"My team was speculating that if Nicolaich was involved, he might have been trying to learn about people from my past that I was close to. Someone he might use for bait, to draw me into a trap. I killed his son on my last mission, and then managed to expose him so that the Russian government was willing to declare him a rogue. We think it's a pretty safe bet that I'm high on his hit list."

"Wait a minute, let's think this through," Parker said. "We know that we were hacked, and our personnel records were gone through, but that was before the attack. The thing is, we didn't find out about the hack until after the attack occurred. It was while they were going through the computers to make sure we were still secure that they found some evidence that someone had been into the system. If we think about just how Machiavellian Andropov seems to think himself to be, then the attack may have been simply a shot fired across the bow. He wanted us to know that he'd already come in through the back door, but we wouldn't find any evidence of it unless he kicked in the front door, first."

"Sir, did anyone actually see Andropov during the attack?"

"We've got two security camera images of a man that could conceivably be him. Facial recognition says it's about an eighty-eight percent match, and the build is right."

"Too bad nobody got a bullet into him," Neil muttered. "Might have ended this whole problem right off the bat."

Noah chewed the inside of his cheek for a moment. "What about casualties on the other side, sir? Did our people manage to take out any of theirs?"

"Oh, yes, we did, we took out seven of them. We even captured three alive, but so far they aren't talking. I'm sure they will, though; we've got a girl down there in interrogation who can be extremely persuasive. If she manages to break him, I'll let you know what we learn."

Noah thanked him, and ended the call. He turned to Moose and Neil.

"Okay, let's assume you're right. Neil, I want you to track down a couple of my old friends. Maybe Nicolaich wants to use them as bait for me, but let's see if we can turn the tables and use them as bait for him."

"No problem, just give me names and somewhere to start."

"Start with Molly Hanson. The last I knew, about a year and a half ago, she was working for Dexter Reedy, the big think tank in DC. She's a super genius and was my best friend when I was a kid. The other one is Jerry Whitehead. He won't be hard to find, he's the lead singer in a big rock group called Reign of Fire. They're the only two I was ever really close to, before you guys. If anybody was going to try to use someone against me, it would be one of them."

"Are you shitting me?" Neil asked. "You actually know Jerry Whitehead from Reign of Fire?"

Noah shrugged. "I can't actually say that I know him now, but I did up until I supposedly killed myself. He and Molly were the two who helped me the most when I was a kid, while I was trying to figure out how to cope with being a Pinocchio in a human world."

Neil rolled his eyes and shook his head, then turned around to the computer and began punching keys. It wasn't long before he was calling off facts and details about both Molly and Jerry, but neither of them seemed to be having any problems at the moment.

"Well, that may shoot that theory down," Noah said. "Of course, either one of them would be pretty hard to get to. Molly is protected by the government, and Jerry would have his own security, I'm sure."

"That wouldn't stop Nicolaich," Sarah said. "And I'll tell you right now, you can forget about Jerry. Nicolaich won't go after him, he'll go after Molly."

Noah cocked his head and looked at her. "Why do you think so?"

Sarah smiled at him. "Because she's a girl. You came after me, didn't you?"

Noah sat there and looked at her for a moment, then turned to Neil. "Is Molly still living in Alexandria?"

Neil nodded while he was still tapping keys. "Yep, a nice place in a gated subdivision. They got their own private security, there, too, and get this: they're part of the Blackstone Group. Those aren't security guards, they're a private army."

Noah nodded. "Yes, but Nicolaich would find a way to go around them, or maybe just go through them. Assuming Sarah is right and Nicolaich would expect me to try to rescue Molly, we can call this a lead. There's nothing that says we have to stay in this cabin, so I guess we'll head for Virginia in the morning. Neil, find the most recent photos you can of Molly and print them out. We'll all need to be watching out for her, so you each need to know what she looks like."

Neil tapped a few keys, and shortly his printer began to hum. While it was working, they began brainstorming about ways to draw Nicolaich out into the open, provided they actually found any sign of him around Molly. That conversation went on through the rest of their dinner, and they had just finished eating when Noah's phone rang.

He picked it up and looked at it, and then answered quickly. "Go ahead," he said.

"Camelot," Doc Parker said. "Allison just came out of surgery. You wanted me to let you know what I found out, so I thought I would call you first."

"Yes, sir?"

"She was apparently struck four times, not three. One bullet struck her in the upper left thigh while two others hit her lower abdomen, causing some intestinal damage. The fourth bullet struck her at an oblique angle on the left side of her head, causing a severe impact to her skull and brain but without penetration. She suffered a rather severe concussion and there may be significant neurological damage. The doctors say she will survive, but it is possible that she will never regain full control of her body. At the moment, it seems that she is unable to speak or to move anything on her right side. They won't know more for a few days, until some of the cranial swelling goes down, but I'll do my best to keep you posted."

"Thank you, sir, I appreciate it. Any word on Mr. Jefferson?"

"Yes. Donald is currently in intensive care at our local hospital. He survived surgery to remove two bullets from his left lung and one that struck him just above and slightly behind his left ear. The doctors say the damage was not as devastating as it could have been, but he is likely to have little or no physical sensation after this. The part of the brain that was damaged is the part that interprets the sense of touch and recognizes pain. They do expect him to survive, but we won't know the extent of the damage for some time, yet."

"That is good news, sir. On our end, we've come to the conclusion that Nicolaich may very well be planning to try using one of my old friends against me, and so we'll be traveling to the area where she resides starting in the morning. I'll let you know if we learn anything else."

"Who is she?" Parker asked. "I can get security on her right now."

"Her name is Molly Hanson," Noah said, "but she'll already have security, and I don't want to tip Nicolaich off, anyway. She works for Dexter Reedy in DC and lives in a secure, gated community in Alexandria."

"In that case, I'll put discrete surveillance on her. If anything happens with her before you arrive, we can let you know about it."

"That sounds like a good idea, sir," Noah said. "It's a long way from here to Alexandria, and we don't know for sure whether Nicolaich is even interested in her. Tomorrow is Sunday and we'll spend it on the road. If he makes a move on her before then, it'll only be to try to draw me in, and we could be completely off target on this. It's just a theory, but it's the only one we've got to go on for right now."

Doc Parker was quiet for a moment, and then he cleared his throat. "Camelot," he said, "I'll get surveillance on her tonight. As for Nicolaich Andropov, if you do find that son of a bitch, I want you to kill him as slowly and painfully as you possibly can. Will you do that for me?"

"Sir," Noah said. "For once, I can honestly say it will be my pleasure."

Noah ended the call and looked up into the faces of the others. "Allison made it through surgery. Apparently she was hit once in the thigh and twice in the gut, but the fourth bullet hit the side of her head hard enough that she may be paralyzed. Doc Parker says they won't know anything more than that for a few days. Donald Jefferson is also alive, but he actually took a bullet in the brain.

They're not sure yet how much damage was done, but they think he'll lose the ability to feel pain or have a sense of touch."

"Well," Sarah said, "at least they're alive."

TEN

Noah's GPS told them it would take twenty-two hours to get to Alexandria, so they were up at five AM to shower and pack. When they left their rooms at five forty-five, Sarah surprised them all by handing the keys to Noah as they got into the car.

"I didn't get nearly enough sleep last night," she said. "You can take on some of the driving today while I kick back and relax. When you get tired, I'll take over."

Noah shrugged and slid behind the wheel. There was a small truck stop situated where the two-lane road met up with Interstate 70, so he stopped there so they could grab some breakfast. The food and coffee were both good and the service was quick, so they were finally on the way at just before seven.

The road was just as boring as it had been the day before, and it wasn't long before Noah was the only one awake. He listened to Neil and Moose snoring in the backseat for a few minutes, then set the cruise control at seventy-five and turned the radio on low so that he could listen to the news reports.

The national news services were almost going into fits. Between the massive explosion in Columbia and what seemed to be some sort of terrorist attack on a small town in Colorado, the announcers were using up all of the most horrific adjectives they could think of.

The FBI had issued a statement the day before regarding the explosion, announcing that all of the victims who'd died in the blast had been identified as members of the Angelos Michoacan drug cartel, and that the explosion was suspected of being the work of a rival cartel. They also found the wreckage of the van in the quarry and were speculating that the perpetrators may have accidentally blown themselves up. The blast was so hot that it was difficult to determine whether anyone had been within range of it.

The attack in Kirkland, on the other hand, seemed to be something of a mystery. The E & E offices were publicly known as the headquarters of Brigadoon Investments Corporation, a privately held company that administered investments of retirement funds for many different companies. The agents handling the investigation had come to the conclusion that Brigadoon had been targeted because of its investments in military technologies. They had no specific suspects, and had not yet managed to tie the attack to any known terrorist groups. Nevertheless, the attacks were being treated as acts of terrorism, which kept them firmly under the jurisdiction of the federal government. Colorado state investigators were complaining that the feds were not bothering to share any information, but the FBI reiterated that acts of terrorism fell under United States jurisdiction, rather than that of any particular state in which they might occur.

"Brigadoon CEO Allison Peterson," said one announcer, "and CFO Donald Jefferson were both wounded in the attack and are currently listed in critical condition at separate hospitals. Nineteen people died in the attacks, and an additional forty-eight were wounded. The military-style attack took place in broad daylight, and authorities believe there were at least fifteen attackers involved. Seven of them died during the attack, after exchanging gunfire with local police and security personnel."

There was no mention of the three attackers who were captured, which told Noah that Doc Parker was keeping that information to himself. He had mentioned to Noah that they had been turned over to E & E's interrogation team, so it was highly unlikely that the FBI even knew they existed. The thought made Noah wonder if the interrogation was making any headway, and he reached into his pocket for his phone.

"Brigadoon Investments, how may I direct your call?"

"Doc Parker, please, Noah Wolf calling."

"Yes, sir, one moment, please." The hold music began playing, but it was less than thirty seconds before the call was picked up.

"Parker," the old man barked. "Little early for you to be calling, isn't it? Or have you got something for me?"

"Just checking in, sir," Noah said. "We're currently on the way to Alexandria, Virginia. That's where my old friend lives, so it's the most logical place to start our search for Nicolaich. I was wondering if your interrogation has turned up any new information."

"Nothing yet. So far, our three guests are proving to be as stubborn as we expected. We do these things in stages, to break down their reluctance, rather than their resistance. The idea isn't to force them to say something they think we want to hear, but to persuade them to tell us what they truly know."

"Yes, sir, I understand. I don't suppose there's any other news?"

"Well, one thing. Allison got her hands on a telephone somehow this morning and called me while I was still in bed. Took me ten minutes to figure out what she was trying to say, but what it boiled down to was to tell you to keep your head down. I explained that you were actively looking for Andropov, and that he's our most likely suspect. She agrees, but she's afraid you'll be walking into a trap."

"I'm glad to hear she's able to talk at all," Noah said. "The way you talked last night, I thought she was paralyzed."

"Only on the right side, but her left hand seems to be working normally. Her speech problem has to do with the fact that only the muscles on the left side of her face are responding at the moment. Like I said, it took a little time to understand her, but there's no doubt that her mind is as sharp as ever. She'll be back in this chair eventually, don't you doubt it."

"That's good news, sir. Please let me know if your interrogators come up with anything. For now, we're just going to proceed with the plan we came up with last night."

"That's fine, and keep me apprised." The line went dead and Noah slipped his phone back into his pocket. He glanced into the rearview mirror and saw that Moose and Neil were still sleeping, then flicked his eyes at Sarah.

She was awake and looking at him. "What's good news?"

"Allison can talk, but she's having problems because her right side is paralyzed. Apparently it makes it hard to understand her, but she got her left hand on a telephone and called Doc Parker at home this morning. She wanted him to tell me to be careful because I'll be walking into a trap."

Sarah's eyes widened and she stared at him for a moment. "I'm assuming the good news you referred to is the fact that she can talk at all, right? Because the thought that she thinks we're going into a trap doesn't sound like very good news at all, not to me."

Noah nodded. "Right. Parker says her mind is as good as it ever was, and that's the important thing. E & E can't afford to lose her. She's not only the brains of the operation, I think she's also its soul. She comes off as coldhearted and dangerous, but I can tell that she agonizes over every decision on whether or not to sanction a hit. It's not that human life doesn't matter to her, it's just that she's strong enough to know that sometimes you just have to eliminate the problem."

Sarah made a sound that Noah took for a snort. "She isn't that cold," Sarah said. "Sometimes, when we're in briefing, she acts more like my big sister than a boss. I mean, look at this engagement ring. I can guarantee you the idea to have us pose as being engaged on this last mission was all hers. She knows I'm crazy about you, so she gave me a little chance to fantasize about what things might be like if we were normal. Somebody coldhearted wouldn't even think of it."

"As long as it doesn't leave you dissatisfied when things go back to the way they are. I'm comfortable with our relationship the way it is, but I'm willing to explore where it could go, if you want. I just don't want to be disappointed if it doesn't feel like that fairytale ending you dreamed about when you were a kid."

Sarah watched him for a moment, then reached across and laid her hand on his arm. "Well, it's like you said. You ain't no Prince Charming, but I'm not exactly Cinderella, either. I'm okay with the way things are; just don't hold it against me if I daydream now and then, okay?"

"Everybody daydreams," Neil said suddenly from the backseat. "What are we daydreaming about today?"

Sarah leaned into the gap between the front seats and smiled at him. "Noah and I are daydreaming about getting married and adopting you. We decided we want children, and you're the most childish person we know."

Neil stared at her for five seconds, and then stuck his tongue out at her. He closed his eyes and leaned against the door and was snoring again only a minute later. Sarah turned her attention back to Noah.

"So, did the old man have anything else for us?"

Noah shook his head. "Not yet. He thinks it will take a little time for the captives to talk. One of the things I like about him is that he doesn't try to torture information out of people, or at least not in any way most people would think of as torture. He said they try to break down reluctance rather than resistance, so nobody's trying to just say what they think we want to hear."

"That makes sense, I guess," Sarah said. "I just wish they'd tell us something, anything to let us know whether we're on the right track or not." She rubbed her hand on his arm for a moment. "So, tell me about this girl we're going to see. You said she was your best friend, but was she more than that?"

Noah glanced at her and then turned his eyes back to the road. "In a way," he said. "We were both unusual, neither of us was the normal teenager. I was the guy who went through puberty without even noticing it, and she was so wrapped up in trying to learn everything she could that she didn't want to take the time to deal with boys. She came up with the idea that if people thought we were a couple, they wouldn't bother either of us, and then she had to explain to me how a boyfriend was supposed to act with his girlfriend."

Sarah's eyebrows were as high as they could go on her forehead. "And how did that work out for you?"

"Pretty well, actually. She taught me about kissing and holding hands and such, and then we started going out on dates together with some other kids who were dating."

"Oh, really? So, this girl we're going to check on was your girlfriend. How long did that last?"

"It was about three-and-a-half years, from the time I was thirteen up until just before I turned seventeen and would have started my junior year in high school. We were together in the same foster home for a couple of years, and then I got sent to live on a farm, so we only got to see each other in school and on weekends after that."

Sarah sat quietly for a moment, and Noah looked over at her briefly. "If you're wanting to know if it was a real relationship, it wasn't. Each of us was just the convenient way out of a bad situation for the other one. She wanted someone to hang out with and do girlfriend things with, and I needed to cover up the fact that I didn't need a girlfriend at all. It was a workable solution. And if you're wondering whether it was a sexual relationship, yes, it was."

Sarah lowered her eyes to her lap. "Did you—I mean, was it like us? Did you love her, the way you were talking about loving me the other night?"

Noah didn't say anything for a moment, and Sarah finally looked up at his face. "Noah?"

"I'm trying to figure out how to explain it," he said. "Molly was my friend, nothing more. When we were pretending to be a couple, it was just that, a pretense. We each needed a camouflage to cover up how we were different from everybody else, so we were obviously the ideal solution for each other." He looked over at her and smiled, then turned his eyes back to the road again. "When I was busy and couldn't see her, it didn't bother me a bit. With you, I've come to the point that when you're not around, I find myself wondering where you are and what you're doing. That may not seem like much of a difference, but from my perspective it's pretty profound."

Sarah still had her hand on his arm, and slid it down to entwine her fingers with his. "I think I understand," she said. "So, when we get there, I don't have anything to worry about?"

Noah's eyebrows lowered and he glanced at her. "Worry about? What do you mean?"

Sarah suddenly laughed. "Never mind," she said. "If you don't understand why I asked, then obviously I don't."

"Could you two keep it down," Neil grumbled. "A few of us are trying to sleep back here."

Sarah looked back to make a face at him, but he hadn't even opened his eyes. She squeezed Noah's hand and leaned back in the seat. It wasn't long before she dozed off and Noah was alone once again.

It was almost eleven before he had to stop for gas, and everyone woke up as he pulled off the ramp. "Gas stop," he announced. "Anybody hungry?"

"I am," Moose said. "Where are we?"

"Almost to Kansas City. There's a half-dozen restaurants here, take your pick."

They chose a small truck stop that had a KFC attached and Noah filled the tank while the rest went inside to use the restrooms and freshen up. When he was finished, he pulled the car up to the building and made his own way in to find the facilities.

Sarah was waiting for him when he came out, but Neil and Moose had already gone over to the restaurant side. There was a buffet and they were already making their ways along it, piling chicken, corn-on-the-cob and other side dishes onto plates that looked like they were about to break. Noah ordered two more buffets for himself and Sarah and they followed the guys to a table near the windows.

Neil was already working on his second drumstick by the time they sat down, and Moose was almost finished with a breast. Sarah stared at them for a second and said, "You guys are pigs."

"Hey!" Neil said. "Moose is a pig, I'm a growing boy! I have to eat to keep up my strength."

Moose put down the bones and looked at Sarah. "He's right, I'm a pig. Especially when it comes to fried chicken." He picked up another breast and bit into it.

ELEVEN

Sarah took the wheel when they got back on the road, and they made good time across Missouri. All four of them fell silent as they passed Columbia, but they were back to their jocular camaraderie just a few minutes later. The trip was long, and they passed the time by talking about many different things.

They stopped for dinner near Indianapolis, grabbing burgers and fries at a McDonald's and eating in the car as they drove. Three hours later, Noah decided they should stop and get a room for the night, so they found a motel in Cambridge, Ohio and got two rooms.

"Everybody get some sleep," Noah said. "We're only about six hours out from Alexandria, so let's plan on hitting the road around eight. That'll put us there midafternoon, give us time to scope out the situation a bit before we contact Molly."

They went into their respective rooms. Sarah waited until the door was shut before she grabbed Noah by the hand and dragged him toward the bathroom. "Shower time," she said, "and then I'm gonna show you why you like me better than your old girlfriend, Molly."

* * * * *

The motel had a continental breakfast set up, so they all met there for waffles at seven fifteen and were out the door and on the road a couple of minutes before eight. Sarah took the wheel and got them back onto the interstate, set the cruise control at eighty and kept up with the heavy truck traffic.

Noah's phone rang at just before eleven, and the caller ID said "Brigadoon Investments." He answered quickly.

"Hello?"

"Camelot, an update," said Doc Parker. "First, you should be getting near your destination by now, am I correct?"

"Yes, sir, about two and a half hours out."

"Very good. Ms. Hanson is under surveillance, as I promised, and at this point we have seen no sign of any threat to her. She went to her office at Dexter Reedy this morning and is still there. I took the liberty of getting her schedule from their security people, so I can let you know that she will be leaving her office at around five this evening, after which she will probably go out for dinner. I'll email you a copy of it in just a moment, along with their security dossier on her, gives you details like her friends and associates, all these, bad habits, etc. Have you decided how you are going to make contact with her?"

"At this point, I'm not planning to make contact at all. What I want to do is put her under our own surveillance, with Sarah, Moose and myself tailing her while Neil does his electronic magic and watches her through all of the electronic eyes out there. I want us to stay out of sight until we know whether or not Nicolaich is even planning anything here. I don't suppose you've gotten anything out of your house guests, have you?"

"One of them has grudgingly admitted that a man fitting Andropov's description seemed to be giving the orders, but that's all we've gotten from him. This fellow is nothing more than an American gun-for-hire who would be spending the rest of his life in prison should we turn him over to the feds, so we've offered to recruit him if he cooperates more fully. He seems to be thinking about it today."

"Sir, are you sure we would want him? He may well have killed some of our people."

"Clandestine agencies often recruit former mercenaries, Camelot," Parker said. "It's not an entirely uncommon practice for their previous sins to be forgiven in the process."

"Understood. Anything new on Allison or Mr. Jefferson?"

"Allison is in a medically induced coma at the moment," Parker said. "The doctors said they couldn't get her to stay quiet long enough to let her brain swelling go down, so they just put her to sleep for a while. Donald, on the other hand, is doing quite well. He does seem to have lost some sensation, it seems, mostly in his chest and legs. They actually had him up walking around yesterday afternoon, and they're saying they expect him to be able to return to work within six weeks."

"That would be good. We'll keep both of them in our thoughts."

"Yes, do that. I'll let you know if I hear anything else." The line went dead.

Noah relayed the information about Allison and Jefferson to the others, and then pointed at a billboard promoting a café at the next exit. "Molly's going to be in her office the rest of the afternoon," he said. "Let's go ahead and grab some lunch now."

Moose and Neil agreed, so Sarah nodded and moved into the right lane so that she could take the exit. A few minutes later, they pulled up in front of Wild Bill's Café and went inside. The restaurant was rustic, reminiscent of something that might have been seen in the Wild West a century and a half earlier, despite modern appliances, menu and prices.

"So," Moose said around the roast beef sandwich he was eating, "I gather we're just going to keep an eye on this girl?"

"That's the plan," Noah said. "If Nicolaich is truly planning to use someone from my past to try to draw me out, then I have to agree with Sarah that Molly is the logical choice. He wants to use her for bait to trap me, but I'd definitely prefer to turn the tables. Dexter Reedy has good security, and apparently so does her subdivision; Nicolaich would be watching her, trying to figure out any pattern that would let him get to her without interference. The idea is for us to watch her, too, and hopefully spot him before he can make his move."

"And if we do? What then?" Neil asked.

Noah looked at each of them in turn. "We take him alive," he said. "I promised Doc Parker that I would make it slow and painful. I plan to do exactly that."

Sarah had been looking into his eyes as he spoke, and suddenly glanced down at the sandwich she was holding. She blinked once, then put the sandwich down on the plate.

"Something wrong, Sarah?" Neil asked her.

She looked up at him for a moment without speaking, then slowly shook her head. "It just hit me," she said. "I've never actually seen anyone die, but after what that son of a bitch did to me in Moscow, I think I want to watch."

"You want to watch? Hell, I want to help. By the way, Boss, did you give any thought to getting me that shotgun?"

Moose's eyebrows tried to crawl over the top of his head. "Shotgun? Neil, as skinny as you are, a shotgun would blast you back to last week. That's like holding a rocket up to your shoulder and setting it off. That's the last thing you need."

"Well, I want something! I can barely even handle a pistol, I always blink and yank it back when I pull the trigger. I can handle a rifle fairly well, but that isn't much good for up close and personal. I need something that's going to wipe out whoever I'm shooting at, you know? I asked the boss to get me a sawed-off."

"Sawed-off shotgun? Well…" Moose seemed to be thinking it over. "Actually, a single-barrel 12-gauge might not be a bad idea. Even if it knocks you on your ass, you'll probably blow away whoever you're shooting at, assuming they're within thirty feet or so. You want to use rat shot, not buckshot. Does a better job of perforating a human body."

Sarah had been watching them as if at a tennis match. "God, the conversations we have while we're eating. Do either of you ever wonder what it would be like to be normal?"

Moose and Neil looked at her for a moment, glanced at each other and then turned back to Sarah. "Nope," they said in unison.

They finished eating and got back into the car for the final leg of the trip.

"I want to find a hotel," Noah said, "and then recon the subdivision Molly lives in before we actually start watching her. I want to know just what kind of security holes we may have to watch out for."

"Neil said security there was Blackstone," Moose pointed out. "Those guys are pretty good, you won't find any. They were trying to recruit me while I was still in SEAL school. Just about all of their people are ex-special forces, and then they get even more training after they sign on."

Noah nodded his head. "You're probably right, I just want to be sure. From what we know of Nicolaich Andropov, if there's any gap in security, he'll spot it. I don't want to give him any opportunity to slip past us."

"Well, if you do find any," Neil said, "I think I can plug them. I've got a dozen dart cameras with me that we can put just about anywhere. We'll need an air rifle, one of the twenty-two caliber ones; Moose can shoot them into walls and such, and they'll transmit high-def video and audio for about a month. They use a multi-frequency setup, splitting up the signals and sending them over four different UHF channels that aren't used anywhere else. If somebody were to pick up one of them, it'd just sound like static, and all we have to do is hide a little receiver that re-combines the signals and streams it to a server back at Neverland. We can watch it live on any computer."

Noah turned and looked back at him. "That's slick," he said. "And I think it might be pretty useful. See if you can find out where to get one of those air rifles, would you? Make it a good one, we need something with both range and accuracy."

"You got it," Neil said as he picked up his computer from the floorboard. A moment later, he and Moose were looking at a web page showing numerous air rifles. "Okay, Boss, there's a Benjamin twenty-two caliber that would be perfect, and we can pick one up at Walmart. In fact…" He tapped a few more keys. "There's one in stock at a Walmart two exits up. We ought to stop and grab it, so that we don't have to go looking for one around Alexandria."

"Good point," Noah said. "Sarah, let's make a stop at Wallyville, shall we?"

Sarah grinned and moved into the right lane. They made the stop at Walmart and were back on the highway only thirty minutes later with the air rifle added to all the other gear in the trunk of the car.

They arrived in Alexandria at just before three. Molly's house turned out to be in a private community known as Gatewood, which consisted of only forty-two homes and was surrounded by a twelve-foot-high brick wall. There were only two entrances, both of which were manned by a quartet of armed guards. Two of them bore only sidearms and would be the ones to approach any vehicle that attempted to enter; the other two carried assault rifles and stayed inside a brick-fenced portico on the guard shack. Moose and Noah spotted them instantly as they drove by.

They circled the compound a couple of times, but Noah didn't want to attempt to get inside while they had a trunk full of weapons and explosives. He took out his phone and googled for hotels, choosing a Holiday Inn Express that was only a mile away. Sarah drove to the hotel and Noah went in to get their rooms.

Their rooms were on the second floor, toward the back of the building. That allowed them to come in through a back entrance and carry all of their gear up without being observed. Moose had been smart enough to get a long, narrow box for the air rifle, but the rest of the guns they carried inside were either small enough to conceal or broke down into manageable components.

They stashed everything inside and took a few minutes to freshen up. Noah told Neil to get out the little Bluetooth-style two-way communicators they used to stay in touch during missions and bring them along. "Just in case we get separated," he said. "We need to be able to stay in touch at all times during this phase of the mission." Noah and Moose checked their pistols and then they all went back to the car. It was time to get in position to start following Molly around.

The offices of Dexter Reedy, the private analysis firm where Molly worked, were in the Woodward building on 15th St. Northwest. Security in the building was very tight, so Noah had Sarah park the car a block away from the main entrance. Molly would be coming out that door a few minutes after five, so that left them with about twenty minutes to wait. Noah passed out the pictures Neil had printed before, so all of them could refresh the mental image they had of her.

It was a good thing they had arrived early, because Molly came out the door five minutes before she should have been getting off work. She stood on the sidewalk for a moment looking up and down the street, and then raised her hand and stepped off the curb as a taxi approached. It screeched to a halt right in front of her and she climbed inside.

"Follow that cab!" Neil said, and then he shrugged. "Sorry, I just always wanted to say that."

Moose and Sarah chuckled while Noah simply raised an eyebrow at him. Sarah put the car in gear and moved smoothly out of the parking space, falling in three cars behind the taxi. The cab appeared to be heading toward Alexandria, at first, crossing the

Potomac on the 14th Street Bridge. Instead of turning south, however, it stayed on Interstate 395 for a couple of miles and then took the King Street exit to the northwest. Sarah changed colors a couple of times, but managed to stay close and keep the cab in sight as it curved onto Leesburg Parkway and finally stopped to let Molly out at an Italian restaurant.

Sarah thought quickly and pulled into the parking lot of the shopping center that surrounded the restaurant. She found a spot that let them keep the front entrance in sight, and the tinted windows on the Chrysler allowed them to watch as Molly paid the driver and turned to go inside.

"Moose, you and Sarah go inside and keep an eye on her. Go ahead and order dinner if she does, you'll need to be able to stay until she's ready to leave. Put your earpieces on so that Neil and I will be able to hear what's going on in there."

Moose chuckled. "This is funny," he said. "Do you know how many times Sarah turned me down for a dinner date before you came along, Boss? Seems kind of ironic that you're ordering us to go on one."

"This is not a dinner date," Sarah said sarcastically. "You're my big brother and you're taking me out for dinner because I'm about to go off to college. Got that?"

One of Noah's eyebrows seemed to pop upward. "That's a good scenario," he said, as Moose laughed again.

Moose and Sarah hung the little headsets on their ears and got out of the car. It wasn't a long walk to the entrance of the restaurant, and they stepped inside less than four minutes after Molly had done so. The hostess smiled up at them as she picked up a pair of menus and showed them to a table that just happened to give them an excellent line of sight to the booth where Molly was sitting with an older gentleman.

A waitress appeared immediately to take their orders, and a couple of minutes were spent as they decided on what to eat, with Sarah gushing about how nice her "big bubba" was to take her out for dinner. When they were done, the waitress took their menus and left.

No one appeared to be paying them any attention, so Moose tapped his earpiece. "Well, it's obvious the girl isn't pining away for you, Boss. She's having dinner with a man who could be Harrison Ford's kid brother, and if the smile on her face is any indication, it isn't a business dinner."

Noah had scanned through the security dossier on Molly that Parker had provided, but now he popped it open again on his phone. There were a number of people listed under "Known Associates," along with photos. It only took him a few seconds to figure out who Moose must be referring to.

"That would be Charles Kitchener," he said. "According to the file, Molly has dinner with him three or four times a month. There's no indication that there's any kind of romance involved, however. He's listed as a Professor of Forensic Psychology at Argosy University. He's also a member of Mensa, so that could be how

Molly knows him. She became a member when she was only nine years old."

"Oh, so that's why the relationship didn't last," Sarah said softly. "She was just too smart for you, huh?"

"She's definitely got the brains," Noah said. "But like I told you, it wasn't a real relationship at all. Just a smokescreen, that's all it was."

"Well, if that's the case," Moose said, "then it probably wouldn't matter if we could overhear the conversation. We wouldn't know what they were talking about, most likely. Besides, I think it's a lot more important for us just to pay attention to who pays attention to her. If our guesses are right, then the bad guy probably has somebody watching her right now, just the way we are."

"Exactly," Noah said. "That's why you're there, to try to spot whoever he's got watching Molly. If we can get a line on who he's using to trail her, then there's at least a chance we can track that person back to our target."

"Kinda have my doubts about that, Noah," Sarah said. "I think he's more the type who would keep his own location a secret even from the people he's working with, at least as far as he can. If he's got someone tailing her, that person won't know where he's at. He'd probably only report by phone, or else he'd simply wait for Nicky boy to contact him."

"I've considered that, too, but right now we have almost no intel at all. If we can at least identify someone working with him, that puts us a little ahead of the game."

"Well, then get ready," Moose said suddenly. "I've got an eyeball on somebody who sure is interested in your old girlfriend."

TWELVE

"Be careful, just observe," Noah said after Moose described the man who was watching Molly like a hawk. "We don't want to tip him off that we're watching her, too. Try not to let him figure it out."

"Boss? She works for that high-powered think tank, right? Could be this guy is just part of their security, keeping an eye on her and making sure she's safe."

"No, I don't think so. The security dossier on Molly says they're fully aware of whatever relationship she has with Kitchener, I don't think they'd be watching her that closely. Of course, we know that Doc Parker has surveillance on her, so it could be one of ours. What do you think of that, Moose? Any chance the guy you're watching is part of our own group?"

"Could be, Boss," Moose said. "I don't know how we can find out for sure, short of walking up and asking him."

"Okay, let me see what I can find out." Noah took out his phone and dialed the home office number. Since it was only three thirty back there, the receptionist answered promptly.

"Brigadoon Investments, how may I direct your call?"

"Doc Parker, please, Noah Wolf calling."

"Yes sir, one moment." Noah had to put up with the hold music for about twenty seconds, and then Parker's gruff voice came on the line.

"Any updates?"

"We're on station," Noah said. "We've taken up surveillance on Molly, and noticed someone else watching her pretty closely. Any chance you can give me an idea of who you've got keeping an eye on her?"

"Give me a moment," Parker said. The hold music returned for nearly a minute and then Parker came back on. "We're using a team of four that we borrowed from DEA. My secretary is sending you the files on them right now, photos and all. We're also sending you their secure cell numbers, and notifying them that they will be under your command from here on out."

"Sounds good," Noah said. "I'll contact them later this evening, and we'll take it from here. I'm hoping it will give us a chance to spot Nicolaich before he can make a move. I want to take him out as quickly as we can. Any updates on the Dragon Lady?"

"Nothing new, she's still in the coma. They're probably going to wake her up tomorrow, but if she can't behave herself, the doctor says she's going right back under. Don Jefferson is doing very well and may get to come home as early as tomorrow. He won't be back at work anytime soon, though."

Noah's phone vibrated in his hand. "Hopefully it won't be too long," Noah said. "I think this outfit needs both him and Allison to keep it headed in the right direction."

"Hey! I don't want this damned job, but I'll do it as long as I have to, and I'll do it pretty damn well, too. You trying to make a comment about my leadership?"

"No, Sir, just making an observation. No disrespect intended, I assure you."

"Oh, that's right, dammit. You're the guy who doesn't know how to be tactful, aren't you? Don't fret about it, son, I'm just a cranky old buzzard. Let me know if there's anything I can do for you from this end."

The line went dead again, and Noah looked at his phone to check the email and files that had just come in. There were photos attached showing three men and a woman. He forwarded it to Moose. "Just forwarded you the files on the four people Parker has watching Molly. Take a look and tell me if that guy in there is one of them."

"Will do, stand by." Noah waited for almost a minute and a half before Moose came back again. "Boss? This guy doesn't match any of those pictures, but the woman in the pictures is sitting three tables over from us right now. She hasn't paid any attention to us, but she isn't giving any to the stalker, either. I don't think it would be obvious to anybody watching that she's watching the girl, but it's possible the other guy has made her."

"Okay, see if you can get a picture of the guy you're talking about."

"Get a picture? How am I supposed to do that without him knowing?"

"Oh, you are such a guy!" Sarah said. "Here, I'll show you. Let me come around beside you..." Noah could hear the sound of chairs shuffling around, and then he heard Sarah's voice again. "Come on, now, we're just going to take a selfie together. Come on, put your arm around me—okay, ready? Got it!"

Noah's phone buzzed again just a few seconds later and he looked at the picture Sarah had sent him. She had aimed the camera over her shoulder to catch the man in the image. The photo showed a tall man, probably in his late 30s. He had dark hair and eyes, and was sporting a thick mustache. Noah passed the phone to Neil in the back seat.

Neil had his computer open on his lap and quickly plugged the phone into it with a connector cord. He downloaded the photo while he was opening a program and quickly cropped out the man's face. "It'll take a little time," he said to Noah, "but I'll start running him through all the facial recognition databases I can. I'm starting off with FBI and CIA, since we're right in their backyard, anyway."

Noah nodded. "Smart thinking," he said. "Moose, try to keep an eye on him without making it obvious. Keep up the small talk between the two of you, talk about this college Sarah's going to, stuff like that. The way you act and talk can be better camouflage than hiding behind the wall."

In the back seat, Neil suddenly called out, "Bingo! Got a match! The stalker is Pasquale Morabito, Italian-American from New York. Thirty-nine years old, got a record for some stupid things when he was younger, assaults and strong-arm robberies. He's been employed four times by mercenary groups and he's still listed as being on the payroll of an outfit called Semaphore Services. They're sort of an anti-terrorist SWAT team, they get sent all over the world when small countries need help dealing with any kind of terrorism."

"Interesting," Noah said. "Any idea how long he's been back in the country since his last job?"

"According to NSA, he was at home in Tennessee until a week ago today. He loaded some gear into a car and drove away, and they lost track of him. No idea where he's been since then."

"This guy works in international military-type circles," Moose put in. "It's a bit of a stretch to think it's only a coincidence that he's sitting here right now, watching the girl we think is a Nicolaich target."

"I absolutely agree," Noah said. "Keep watching, we need to know just how closely he's watching her."

"Hey, Boss?" Neil asked. "Guess what I found."

Noah turned to look at the skinny kid. "What?"

"The cloud-based video stream from the security cameras inside that restaurant. Wanna watch?"

Noah opened his door and then climbed into the back seat beside Neil. His computer monitor was split into four camera views, and one of them showed Molly and her companion.

"Only four cameras?" Noah asked. "I don't see Moose and Sarah on any of them."

"There's a dozen cameras," Neil replied, "but if I split the screen any more we won't be able to make out any details. Here, let me get picky on the cameras I display." He tapped the keys and touch pad for a moment and two of the views changed. Moose and Sarah were centered in one of them and Pasquale Morabito in the other. "How's that?"

Noah nodded appreciatively. "Good job. Moose, Sarah, I'm watching Molly's body language and she seems pretty upset about something. Are you picking up anything in there?"

"Not really," Moose said. "Looks to me like she's smiling a lot."

"I can see that she's smiling, but she's got her hands under the table instead of on top of it, and both feet are flat on the floor. That's the posture of somebody who's unhappy about being where she is, and might be expecting trouble. Wait a minute." Noah leaned closer to the monitor and watched as Molly picked up her purse, which had been sitting toward the outer edge of the seat beside her, and moved it to her other side. "Sarah, get up and head for the ladies' room. Molly will be going there in just a moment."

On the monitor, they watched as Sarah got up and began walking toward the restrooms. Five seconds later, Molly did the same.

"Boss, how did you know?" Moose asked.

"Observation," Noah said. "She moved her purse to the other side of herself so she could slide out of the booth. If she had been planning to get up and leave, she would've picked it up and held it. When she set it down on the inner end of the booth, I knew she was only planning to be gone for a few minutes. Logically, that meant a trip to the ladies' room."

Inside the bathroom, Sarah had taken advantage of the break to make a hurried stop in one of the stalls. She heard the door open as Molly entered, and then another stall door opened and closed. When she finished, she stepped out to the sink and washed her hands, then fidgeted with her hair until Molly came out of her own stall and stepped up to the sink beside her.

Molly washed her hands quickly, then turned and looked at Sarah. "You and your boyfriend keep looking over my way," she said. "Just thought I'd let you know, I'm not into those kind of games."

Sarah's eyes went wide and she spun her face to look at Molly. "Games?" she croaked out. "Um, I'm sorry if I gave you any kind of weird impressions…"

"Then you're following me," Molly said. "That seems to be a popular pastime the last few days. So far, I've counted thirteen different people who seem to like following me around. Most of them are men, and that makes it hard to confront them the way I'm doing with you right now. You want to tell me what's going on, or should I just push the panic button that I carry in my pocket. Trust me, you don't want to deal with the guys who would come running."

Sarah's eyes were even wider than before as she tried to think of something to say. "Look, I don't know…"

"Don't try to play games with me, sweetie," Molly said. "I have to take a refresher course in surveillance recognition every three months, it's part of my contract. Believe me when I tell you I know surveillance when I see it. On the other hand, you're obviously not with the other two guys in there that are watching me. Both of them have been identified as guns for hire, and we've already got people watching them. You're not part of that group, though, I can tell. You've been watching me, but you've also been paying close attention to one of those two guys; that selfie trick was pretty obvious, you didn't even have the phone pointed at yourself. Looked to me like you were getting a photo of that guy, and then you sent it to someone. So cut the shit and tell me who you're working for, or you're going to end up in one of those nasty little rooms in the basement of the Pentagon before this night is over."

"Um…"

Noah's voice suddenly spoke up in her ear. "Hand her the earpiece," he said.

Sarah breathed a sigh of relief as she reached up to her ear and lifted off the little Bluetooth-style earpiece and handed it to Molly. "Put that on for a minute," she said. "I think you'll start to understand things."

Molly looked the earpiece over and then slipped it onto her own ear. "Hello?"

"Don't say any names, just in case you're bugged," said a voice in her ear. "This is your old Vulcan friend, do you recognize my voice?"

It was Molly's turn to have eyes the size of saucers. "Oh my—is it really you?"

"It's me. Long story, and I don't have time to go into it right now, but I work for a government agency you probably never heard of, and that girl and the guy with her are part of my team. I sent them in to watch you because I have reason to believe you may be in some danger."

"What about the other bunch that's been watching me? Are they with you, too?"

"Some of them are working with us, four of them. As for the rest, we believe they're working for the man I'm after. He's trying to draw me out into a trap, and we have a theory that he may try to use you as bait. We're hoping to catch him before he can act on his plans, so that means we have to keep you in sight at all times."

"For what it's worth, I knew you weren't dead. Suicide is not logical, you'd never have taken your own life. That meant somebody faked it, to get you out of Leavenworth. CIA?"

"Molly, I'm sorry, but I'm not sure you have a high enough clearance for me to answer that."

Molly's eyes flicked to Sarah. "Does your team know all about you? The things I know?"

"Yes, they know it all. It's one of the reasons I was recruited."

"I figured they probably did, since you're the one who's using me as bait now. Most people would get upset about that, seeing as how we're old childhood friends. They'd have to understand you, or they probably couldn't work with you."

"Yeah, it caused me some problems at first, but they finally caught on. Question: are you leaving the restaurant with your date?"

"No, we just get together for dinner once in a while. It's not like that. I'll have the restaurant call me a cab when I'm ready to leave."

"I've got a better idea," Noah said. "I think it's time to show myself. When you go back to your booth, make a point of telling your date that you ran into an old friend—her name is Sarah, by the way—and you're going to hang out with her after dinner. Point her out when she comes back to the table, and when you get done eating, just come on out with her and Moose. We'll drive you home, which will let the men watching you get a look at me. For now, you need to get back to your date, you've been gone long enough. And Molly? Trust me when I say we'll do everything we can to keep you safe."

Molly nodded. "I know that," she said, "as long as it doesn't interfere with your mission, right? Don't answer that, I already know. I'm giving this back, now." She lifted the earpiece off her ear and passed it back to Sarah. "Okay, I trust him, so I'll trust you. See you after dinner." She glanced at herself in the mirror and then turned and walked out of the restroom.

Sarah slipped the earpiece back on. "I thought you didn't want her to know you were around?"

"She made you and Moose, so it was the best way to handle the situation. Wait a few more seconds and then go back out to join him. Moose, did you copy all that?"

"I did. She just slid back into the booth, but not before she took a good look at me."

"Yeah, I see her again. I think you guys were what was making her nervous; her body language is nice and calm, now."

Noah watched as Sarah took a seat at the table again, and noticed that Morabito was looking her way as she did so. "Watch Pasquale," he said. "He got suspicious because the two of you were gone so long. I think he's made you."

Molly turned and gave Sarah a finger wave, and Sarah returned it. Molly was smiling as she pointed Sarah out to Kitchener, and Morabito seemed to relax a bit.

Their waitress appeared then, bringing their plates and refilling their glasses. Moose and Sarah dug in to eat, doing their best to avoid paying any attention to Molly or her stalker. Molly's dinner had arrived while she and Sarah were in the ladies' room, and she and Mr. Kitchener were also concentrating on the meal.

THIRTEEN

Neil had gotten hungry while they were waiting, so Noah sent him to get sandwiches from a fast food restaurant across the street. While he was gone, Noah called Parker to fill him in on the change of plans.

"She made us," he said when Parker answered. "Molly figured out that Moose and Sarah were watching her, and confronted Sarah in the bathroom at the restaurant. I decided the best option was to let her know that I'm here, and what the situation is. I didn't go into detail about who I work for."

"The girl has a top-secret clearance, and we occasionally employ Dexter Reedy when we run into problems we can't solve on our own. It's quite possible your old friend already knows something about us. You've got free rein on this, Camelot. Do what you feel necessary."

"Yes, Sir. We'll be driving her home after dinner tonight, so there's a good chance Nicolaich's people will spot me. That's what I'm hoping for, at this point. If he knows I'm in town, he might try to switch over onto me, rather than her."

"Just be sure he doesn't get a clear shot," Parker said. "With the shape we're in, I can't afford to lose you right now."

"I understand, Sir, and I have no intention of letting him win. He wants to turn this into a game but he doesn't realize that all games of skill are based on logic. When it comes to games, I tend to excel."

"That's what I'm counting on, Camelot."

The line went dead, so Noah put the phone away. Neil returned only a moment later and they ate in the car.

The two of them watched the monitor as Moose, Sarah and Molly finished their meals. Moose and Sarah were done first, and waited a few extra minutes for Molly, but finally Noah saw them all rise and start toward the door. He got back into the front passenger seat as the three of them came out of the restaurant and walked toward the car.

"Stalker is on the move," Neil said. "Pasquale waited until our bunch got outside and then headed for the door, himself. He should be stepping out right about—*now!*"

Noah opened his door and stepped out, looking toward the door of the restaurant. Morabito and another man were standing there, and Morabito seemed to be watching Molly, but his eyes locked on Noah's face instantly when Noah stood erect. The two men looked each other in the eyes for the seconds it took for Molly to slide into the backseat between Moose and Neil, and then Morabito and his companion turned and walked toward a car that was parked near the entrance.

Noah got back inside as Sarah started the car, and they were moving only a couple of seconds later.

"Turn right," Noah said. Sarah did as he instructed, which took them past the restaurant's driveway entrance as Morabito was pulling out. He fell in behind them but drove slowly, so that another car got between them only a few moments later.

"Fish took the bait, Boss," Neil said. "They're in the second car back."

"I see him," Noah said, looking into the mirror on his side of the car. "One of them is on the phone, so everyone stay alert."

"Okay, Noah, it's time to tell me what's going on. Who is it you're using me as bait for? And don't give me any of that security clearance crap, I'm cleared for Top Secret, Restricted Access. It don't get any higher, Hotshot."

Noah turned in the seat to look at her. "His name is Nicolaich Andropov. He's a former official of the SVR in Russia, the guy who handled sanctioning assassinations. He and I had a little run-in a few weeks back, and he seems to be the kind of guy who carries a grudge."

Molly was nodding. "Nicolaich Andropov," she said. "He headed up the 'Eraser' division at SVR. He went rogue about two months or so back, had his rank and his entire operation stripped from him because he used agency assets on a personal vendetta mission. The way we got it, he was going after what he believed to be an American agent who killed his son during an operation to rescue the daughter of the president of Mauritania. I'm gonna go out on a limb, here, and guess that you are that agent?"

Sarah glanced at Noah. "Crap, she's good."

"I'm the agent," Noah said. "How do you know so much about it?"

"DR gets called in on a lot of national security issues, and apparently the NSA was scared to death you were going to end up leaving us exposed in Moscow. They didn't tell us who you were, just gave us a codename and the background information on the CIA rescue mission. On the other hand, rumors up on Capitol Hill say that it wasn't CIA at all, but E & E. Now that I know it was you, I think I believe the rumors."

Neil let out a low whistle. "Boss, she must have one hell of a clearance."

"What do you know about E & E?" Noah asked. "That's generally limited to need-to-know."

Molly grinned. "Up until today, all I knew was that they exist. Rumor says you guys might have been involved in that big explosion in Missouri last week. Any truth to that?"

"Need-to-know," Noah said. "I'll concede you have enough clearance to know what we're up to, but I'm not going to give you any other information. I wasn't even planning on letting you know I was here until you called Sarah out in the bathroom. I had sent her in there to strike up a conversation and try to get some idea why you seemed so tense when you were sitting in your booth, but you beat her to the punch. At that point, I just figured it was best to bring you in on it."

"Well, I…" Molly began, but Sarah cut her off.

"Noah, two more cars just fell in with our friend back there, one behind him and one right beside. I get the feeling they're working together and waiting for something. The last time I saw a maneuver like this, it was some undercover cops trying to catch me and my dad in a pincer move. If I'm right, somebody's going to be cutting us off up ahead any second now."

"Then get us out of here," Noah said. "Let's shake them up."

Sarah grinned evilly, and pushed down slightly on her accelerator. The car moved ahead quickly, leaving the three followers behind for several seconds, before they caught on. All three of them suddenly floored their own gas pedals, and a second later they were rapidly gaining on the Chrysler.

Moose reached an arm around Molly and pulled her down suddenly so that she was below the line of sight through the back window. At the same moment, Molly yanked the steering wheel to the left and cut onto a side street. The three pursuers were moving too fast to make the turn, but only one of them slammed on brakes. A moment later, that car reversed, then pulled into the street and began flying toward them.

Sarah had no choice but to slow down when she came to the end, because she couldn't see whether anything was coming. That gave the single car a chance to get a bit closer, but then she floored the Chrysler again and roared out and to the left. By the time the follower got to the corner, she had already turned right at the next intersection and was out of sight. She hit a color button and the car went from its normal silver to a bright green.

The powerful car was making eighty miles an hour through the streets of what appeared to be a residential neighborhood, squealing around corner after corner as Sarah drove a random path in order to throw off their pursuers. After five minutes of such driving, she suddenly slowed to the speed limit and made three more turns in quick succession.

"We lost them," she said. "Now I just want to get away from here quietly before the cops show up."

Moose let Molly sit up again, and she stared at him for a few seconds. "Just so you know," she said, "any other man who shoved my face into his lap like that would have gotten a taste of my pepper spray. Since you're with Noah, I gave you the benefit of the doubt this time, but don't try it again." She turned to Noah. "Does she always drive like that?"

"That's her job," Noah said. "Sarah is one of the best drivers in the whole world, and she can handle just about anything that has wheels. She doesn't have to drive that way very often, but I'm glad she can when it's necessary."

Molly looked at Neil. "Okay, and what about these two back here? One looks like a string bean, and the other looks like he ought to be playing football."

"The quarterback is Moose, he's my backup man. That skinny kid on the other side is Neil, and he could probably give you a run for your money in the IQ department. According to our bosses, he's got the highest IQ they've ever seen, and he can pull intelligence out of thin air with a computer. He hacked into the security cameras at that restaurant, and that's how I was able to watch you. I don't think we've found anything yet that he couldn't find out, if I asked him to."

Molly was nodding again. "A three-man support team, right? Transportation, intel and muscle. I've seen a paper on the advantages of espionage teams built that way, but I didn't know any of our alphabet soups were using it. You're E & E, right? Did I get it right?"

"He could tell you," Moose said, "but then he might have to kill you. And if you know the Boss, you know he'd do it."

Molly's eyes shot open wide and she stared at Moose. "Good point," she said. "Noah, forget I asked."

Sara switched the car back to its original silver color and took a different route back to Molly's place. She wasn't surprised to see one of the three cars that had been following them sitting outside the gate that led into the subdivision. She pointed it out to Noah, who nodded.

"I see them," he said. "I would have been surprised if they weren't waiting for us here, but they won't make a move on us here, not with the security on this place."

Sarah pulled in and stopped at the gate, and the guard on duty stepped out to the car.

"Good evening," he said politely. "How can I help you this evening?"

Molly leaned forward. "Hey, Ray," she said. "These are some friends of mine, they're giving me a ride home."

Ray looked the other occupants of the car over, then smiled at Molly. "Okay, Ms. Hanson," he said. "Oh, by the way, I'm supposed to get your signature on a receipt for something that got delivered today. Could you come inside the guard shack for a moment?"

Molly rolled her eyes. "Sure, Ray, no problem." She turned to Moose. "Open up, Muscles," she said. "They're not going to let us pass here until I go inside and assure them you're not holding a gun to my head."

Ray grinned as Moose opened the door and stepped out, allowing Molly to get out as well. "Sorry, folks, it's our protocol, and I have to follow it. Everything I do here is being videotaped and recorded, and I happen to like my job."

Noah smiled at him. "Trust me, I understand completely. You need to frisk us?"

"No, that's okay. As long as she's able to get out of the car and step inside, it's a pretty safe bet you're not forcing her to take you in with her." Ray followed Molly into the guard shack, where she could be seen through the windows smiling and talking with the other guards. A moment later, he escorted her back to the car. "Okay, folks, you can go on in. And by the way, I appreciate your cooperation."

"Not a problem," Sarah said, and Noah nodded his agreement. As soon as Molly and Moose were settled back into the car, she put it back in gear and eased through the opening gates.

"Sorry," Molly said. "I should have warned you about that. This whole complex is owned by DR, and they get pretty sticky about security."

"Yes, but under the circumstances, that's a good thing," Noah said. "Nicolaich isn't one who would be stopped for very long by your average security company, but these guys are professional enough to make him stop and think it over. Let's get you home, then we'll go play cat and mouse with whoever's in that car out there."

"Wait a minute," Molly said, her eyes wide. "You think you're just gonna drop me off and leave? I don't think so. You guys are coming in and filling me in on what's going on here. I want to know everything."

"I'll fill you in," Noah said, "but not tonight. Right now, it's extremely critical that the watchdog out there at the gate sees us leaving. There's no doubt in my mind that they're reporting directly to Nicolaich, and what I'm hoping is that he'll decide to leave you alone and come after me, now that he knows I'm here."

Molly glared at him. "Fine, but come by my office tomorrow, we can talk freely there. Make it about 10 o'clock, will that work? I'm guessing you're not using your own names, right now, so what names should I put on the approval list?"

Neil produced a notepad and pen and wrote down the four names they were using for her. She stuffed the note into her purse as Sarah maneuvered through the subdivision. Noah noticed four Blackstone Security SUVs patrolling the streets, which told him there were probably several more he hadn't seen. The homes were townhouse-style, each one sharing an adjoining wall with at least one other unit. The GPS in the dashboard led Sarah directly to Molly's place and she pulled into the driveway.

"Okay," Molly said as she got out of the car. "Don't forget, 10 AM. I'll make sure no one else is around, so we can talk."

Noah nodded. "We'll be there. Maybe you can help us figure out how to handle this whole situation."

They waited until Molly was inside, then drove away. As they passed through the gate and turned right, the dark sedan pulled away from the curb and followed them.

"Want me to lose them?" Sarah asked. "Or no?"

"Let them follow us for a bit, but don't go back to the hotel just yet. Let's take a ride up to Arlington and shake them there."

Sarah grinned as she headed for the interstate.

While Sarah took care of their shadows, Noah called up on his phone the files on the four DEA agents. He called them one by one, introduced himself as Camelot and then instructed them to await his further orders.

FOURTEEN

When your car can change color, it's not hard to avoid being noticed by people looking for a particular shade. They got back to the hotel without picking up another tail, and gathered in Noah and Sarah's room.

"There's no doubt Nicolaich knows we're here, now," Noah said. "I'm sure those guys managed to snap a few pictures of us, and I'm sure Nicolaich will recognize us easily. From here on out, we need to stay alert and ready for anything. Neil, I have to give you a weapon, but I haven't had a chance to look into that shotgun." He reached into a bag sitting on the dresser and produced one of the MP9 machine pistols, along with a pair of long, stick-like magazines. "I think this will do for now. It's a full auto pistol, but it's set for three-round bursts, which means you'll fire three shots every time you pull the trigger. If you've got it pointed at someone, there's a good chance at least one of those rounds will hit him."

Neil's face lit up in a big grin. "Excellent!" he said. "I've fired one of these at the range, I know how to handle it. And yeah, I hit the target more often with it."

"Sarah, I know you're pretty good with your pistol, but there's another of those if you want it."

She shook her head. "Daniel says my little hands are the reason my Beretta is perfect for me. It's got a smaller grip than most pistols and I can actually get a squeeze on the trigger. I'm accurate enough with it up to fifty yards, and anybody trying to get to me will probably be within fifty feet. If I can get a shot at them, I can hit them."

Noah nodded and looked at Moose. "It should be dark enough now," he said. "Take the airgun and put some of Neil's little cameras out where we can keep an eye on the parking lot and the lobby."

Moose started to get up, but Neil stopped him. "The dart cameras are okay for outside, but I doubt you can get one in the lobby without being noticed. However, since I'm a genius, I still have a few of the little sticker microphones we used before. If you stick a couple of them up in the lobby, I've got a program that can listen for keywords. If I put in all of our names, including our real names and fake ones, it will sound off if anybody comes in asking about us."

"That sounds good," Moose said. "Give me a couple of them, and a couple of the dart cameras." He picked up the air rifle as Neil opened his bags to get the gadget, then opened the door and peeked into the hallway before slipping out. He was back in less than ten minutes. "Got one camera facing the parking lot entrance, and one focused right on our car. The microphones are in place in the lobby, too, one of them stuck under the lip of the front desk and the other on the wall by the door."

Neil pushed a button on a small black box and then turned to his computer. A couple of minutes later, he had a split screen showing the views from the two cameras, and had told the computer to listen to the microphones for their names.

"That's as close as we can get to setting up a perimeter of security," Noah said. "Neil, you take first watch while Moose gets some sleep. Wake him up in four hours and let him take over. Moose, that will put your shift ending at about seven. We'll plan on going down for breakfast around seven thirty."

Moose and Neil left the room, taking the computer with them. As soon as they were gone, Sarah got up and began stripping. "I'm headed for the shower," she said. "Come with me?"

Noah didn't answer, but stood up and began taking off his own clothes. The bathroom simply had a tub with a shower curtain, and it was a little tight. They spent a couple of minutes just holding each other under the spray.

"Noah, I'm scared," Sarah said. "Nicolaich is good, we probably won't see them coming."

Noah pulled her a little tighter to his chest. "It's me he wants most," he said. "And he seems to be just a little bit crazy about it. Crazy people make mistakes, that's what I'm counting on. We're going to get him this time. I want him dead so that he can't ever cause us problems again."

Sarah held onto him for another moment, then let go and turned to pick up the bottle of body wash. Noah took it from her hands and squeezed it into one of his own.

* * * * *

The hotel had a continental breakfast, but none of them were in the mood for waffles that morning. Neil had studied the view from the two little cameras and concluded that no one was sitting outside, watching for them, so they walked out and got into the car. The GPS said there was a Bob Evans restaurant not far away, and Sarah started in that direction.

They sat at a table so that each of them could watch in a different direction as they ate. The breakfast was good and they lingered over it for a bit, finally leaving at just before nine. The drive into DC took most of an hour, so they arrived at the Dexter Reedy office building just a few minutes ahead of schedule.

Sarah found a parking space that was almost in front of the entrance, and they walked inside. Two security guards at a desk in the lobby looked up with smiles on their faces.

"Good morning," one of them said. "Can we help you?"

Noah smiled back. "Yes, I'm Wyatt Wilson, I have an appointment to see Molly Hanson this morning."

"No problem, could I see some identification, please?"

All four of them produced the IDs they were using and the guard looked at them as he scanned a list of scheduled visitors on the computer. Satisfied, he handed them back and then passed each of them a visitor's badge on a lanyard.

"Just hang those around your necks," he said. "I'll call Ms. Hanson and she'll be down to get you in just a moment."

They did as they were told and Molly appeared only a couple of minutes later, stepping out of an elevator. "Yoohoo," she called. "Come on up."

They followed her into the elevator and she pushed the button for the fifth floor. "How's the sky looking out there?" she asked. "There's a rumor going around that there might be a storm coming."

Sarah blinked. "Looked pretty clear to me," she said, and then it dawned on her that Molly was actually asking whether the situation was likely to blow up anytime soon. "But you never know, sometimes lightning can strike out of what looks like a clear blue sky."

"Don't I know it," Molly said. "I swear, sometimes things you just couldn't possibly expect come at you from your blind side. It's a weird feeling, almost like somebody coming back from the dead, you know?"

The twinkle in her eyes caused Sarah to smile, but she didn't respond. The elevator stopped and opened, and they followed Molly down the long hallway and into a conference room. She closed the door behind them and then held up one finger as she crossed the room to a cabinet that held a coffee urn. She opened a drawer that was apparently full with an electronic device of some sort, pushed the button on it and then turned back to face Noah.

"Okay, we're secure. That's a signal generator that can jam any transmitter within a hundred yards, so nobody's going to be listening in on us. Let's sit down, shall we?"

All three of the men got themselves a cup of coffee, but the girls declined. Once they were all seated, Noah began to explain to Molly how he had been railroaded by the Army's justice system and then recruited by E & E. He told her about the mission that took him to Russia to rescue a kidnapped girl, and how Nicolaich had been stripped of his authority in Russia and gone rogue after trying to get revenge on Noah for the death of his son. She listened with rapt attention as he told her about the mission that had led to the situation they were in, and then about the attacks on Neverland.

Molly listened in silence until Noah was finished, then leaned back in her chair and rubbed her eyes. "So Uncle Sam found a way to turn your problems into an asset. Not surprising. Noah Foster, super assassin: almost sounds like a movie."

Noah shrugged. "Noah Foster is dead," he said. "He died in the prison cell in Leavenworth, and I was resurrected. My name is Noah Wolf, now, and that's partly because of you. You're the one who showed me that I was a lot like a wolf, remember?"

She grinned. "Oh, I remember. We were at Mrs. Connors' house." She suddenly leaned forward and put her chin in her hand, her elbow on the table supporting it. "Now look at you. You're a wolf in sheep's clothing. You look like one of us, you act like one of us, you move among us completely unnoticed—but all the time you're simply waiting for the chance to strike." She sat back again and shook her head. "Andropov—he's after you personally, right?"

"It appears that way," Noah said with a nod. "The thing I don't understand in all this is why he attacked Neverland. According to everything we've been able to learn, he already got into the personnel files before that happened. He would have already found everything he needed to try to come after me."

"You're not looking at it the right way," Molly said. "He's not just after revenge, he wants to hurt you even worse than you hurt him. Look at the things he's done up to now." She pointed at Sarah. "He abducted this girl and used her for bait to draw you into a trap, but you managed to turn the tables on it. He tried to use his Russian agents and assassins to take you all out, but that only led to him being exposed as a rogue factor, someone they could control. He was ousted, so to his mind he's lost everything that was important to him. He can survive in the world just fine; I mean, he's got God knows how much blackmail material on God knows how many powerful people, so he can make a lot of money trading in information, assassinations, whatever his market happens to be looking for."

Noah was nodding as he looked into her eyes. "So, you're saying that's what he wants to do to me, take away everything that's important to me."

"Yep. You thought he was planning to kidnap me to use as bait, the way he used Sarah the last time, but that wouldn't make sense. If he really got your files, he knows that you won't be tricked into sacrificing yourself over some emotional attachment to your old friend Molly. That wouldn't work, and he'd know it. What did work, though, is that he made you think that's what he wants so that you'll turn those tables again, and it worked: you didn't come here to protect me as much as to use me to help you get to him."

"That isn't fair," Sarah said suddenly. "As soon as I pointed out that Nicolaich was more likely to come after you than anybody else, Noah was all about getting here to make sure you were safe, even had surveillance put on you until we could arrive."

Molly turned to face her. "Oh, my God, you're in love with him," she said. "Look, Sarah, I'm not pissed at him for wanting to use me as bait, but you need to understand that I know how he works. I psychoanalyzed him when we were kids, I'm the one who taught him to mimic the way other people act so that he wouldn't end up in an institution somewhere. I'm not saying there isn't some part of him that's willing to do what it takes to keep me alive, but I know him. His mission—whether it's a government mission or one that he sets for himself—is always going to be more important to him than I am, and right now, that mission is to kill Nicolaich Andropov. If I happen to be in the way, if Nicolaich threatened to kill me if Noah didn't back down or surrender, Noah would simply consider my death to be collateral damage to the mission. You might as well wrap your head around that, because the same would be true for each of you. If he's put in the position of having to choose between saving you or accomplishing his mission, the mission is going to win. He might feel some kind of regret that he lost you, but that Vulcan brain of his is hardwired to do whatever has to be done."

"They know that," Noah said. "You're absolutely right, my original plan was to simply tail you until Nicolaich made his move, then try to take the bastard out. I would have done what I could to keep you out of the line of fire, for whatever that's worth."

"Of course you would've, because that would be logical. Avoid collateral damage if possible, right? Noah, I understand. The thing is, I get paid a ridiculously high salary because some of my professors figured out that I have an extremely analytical mind. I seem to have developed the ability to combine lots of random bits of information and come up with a pretty good prediction of what's going to happen. Looking back, I probably owe a lot of that to you. Trying to keep you out of trouble meant always being one step ahead of everybody else. I had to watch everything so that I could predict where the next problem would come from."

Noah nodded. "I remember," he said. "You kept everybody else from figuring out what a mess I really was."

Molly made a sad smile and looked at Sarah. "See what I mean? He acknowledged what I said, but it never even occurred to him to feel any gratitude. He just doesn't have that part of the normal human programming." She turned back to Noah. "The thing is, when I apply that analytical mind of mine to the things you've told me, I get a picture of what is likely to happen. You showed up here, just like Nicolaich thought you would. His people have reported back to him that you have arrived, so he'll be looking at putting his next phase into operation. The first thing he'll want to do is make sure you understand that he isn't playing any games, this time."

Noah cocked his head to the side and looked at her. "Then he's going to try to kill you. You weren't in any actual danger until I got here, but now that I am, he'll try to kill you as a way of sending me that message."

"No doubt about it," Molly said. "He's probably already got it in motion, and it's not likely I'll be able to spot it in time to duck."

Noah looked at her for a moment. "I've got four DEA agents on loan, so I'm going to put them on you as personal security, two at a time." He took out his phone and called two of the agents immediately, telling them to come directly to the Dexter Reedy office building. "First shift will be a man and a woman, Bill Lassiter and Carmen Sanchez. Both of them will be armed and Ms. Sanchez will be staying with you even if you go to the bathroom. Combined with your own security, they should be able to keep you alive. We'll be taking another tack on this, to see if we can get to Nicolaich before he gets to you."

Molly grinned. "Well, I certainly hope you can," she said. "You owe me, Noah, for all the crap I had to put up with when we were kids. You keep this guy from killing me and I'll be happy to call it even." She turned her eyes to Sarah. "As for you, I don't know whether to cheer you on or warn you off. Knowing Noah and his habit of being ridiculously honest, I'm sure you're fully aware that I was the first girlfriend he ever had, so I know exactly what you go through."

Sarah looked startled. "He told me, but the way he said it was that it wasn't a real relationship, just a way to keep people from wondering about the two of you."

Still grinning, Molly said, "Of course that's what he told you, because that's what I told him at the time. We were in our early teens, if I had told him that I was in love with him he would've wanted me to explain those feelings, and I didn't have a clue how to do that. It was easier just to tell him it was all a pretense. I got what I wanted, which was him doing everything he could to act like my boyfriend, and he didn't have to worry about trying to fit into the teenage romance scene. I was crazy about him, of course, but I don't think he ever knew that."

Sarah was looking from Molly to Noah and back. "Are you still…"

The grin spread even wider and suddenly burst into laughter. "Am I still in love with him? Good Lord, no! We kept up that relationship for close to four years, and by the time it was over I was having to force myself to keep up the act. It wasn't that I didn't like him anymore, it was just a matter of being tired of keeping up a pretense for so long. Two weeks after I moved away I had a brand-new boyfriend, one who thought I was the dream girl he'd been looking for all his life. There's a big difference between someone kissing you because it's 'appropriate,' and someone kissing you because he wants to so badly he can't see straight. Sooner or later, you're going to realize that Noah can't give you what you really want and need. It isn't his fault, he just doesn't have it in him."

Sarah stared into her eyes for a moment, her own face showing that she was controlling her anger. "Let me tell you something," she said. "A couple of months back, Nicolaich Andropov managed to infiltrate our group and kidnap me. I'm the one he used as bait that time, to draw Noah into a trap where he planned to kill him. Noah knew that, knew good and well that coming to get me would probably get him killed, but he came anyway. Maybe he doesn't have feelings the way the rest of us do, but when we were all being debriefed and he got asked why he came after me even though it violated protocol, do you know what he said? He said he came after me because he didn't like the thought of a world that existed without me in it. Just because he never had those feelings for you, don't you sit there and try to tell me he can't have them for me. I know I'm expendable, I know that if it came down to me or the mission, the mission would probably win, you're right about that. But at least I know that up to that point, he'll do anything it takes to protect me." She leaned forward until her face was only inches from Molly's. "Now, if that isn't some kind of love, then you tell me what it is."

Molly's grin was gone, replaced by the sad smile she had used earlier. "In his case, Honey, it's simply selfishness. He obviously enjoys you, and he doesn't want that enjoyment to come to an end, so he'll do his best not to let you get away. But if you do—if he loses you, no matter how it happens, he'll move on without ever suffering any grief or remorse. As long as you can handle that, then maybe you can survive being in love with Pinocchio."

FIFTEEN

Lassiter and Sanchez showed up a half hour later and were introduced to Molly. They were informed about Andropov and the likelihood that he was planning to kill Molly, and Noah made it clear that he expected them to do everything possible to keep that from happening. Both of them seemed quite dedicated to their duties, and to have the skills necessary to accomplish their goals.

"Okay," Noah said, "it's time for us to go do a little tree shaking. Molly, we'll be in touch later. You stick with your bodyguards while we do everything we can to take Nicolaich down."

"And what are you gonna be doing?" Molly asked.

"I think it's time we turn the tables a bit. He's got people watching you, now watching us whenever they can; they think they got the easy job, so I think it's time we engage them."

The team left the building and walked to the car. Moose and Noah spotted a Ford sedan parked at the end of the block at the same time.

"Three men in that Ford," Moose said. "They're eyeballing us pretty intently."

"I see them. Let's take them for a cruise in the countryside." They slid into the car and Noah turned to Sarah. "Just head toward Clifton. We're looking for somewhere isolated."

Sarah looked at him and swallowed hard, then punched "Clifton, Virginia," into the GPS and put the car in gear. Noah pulled down the sun visor and used the vanity mirror to watch the Ford pull out behind them.

Sarah pulled the car onto Interstate 66 a few moments later and the Ford followed them up the ramp. The driver was carefully keeping them in sight, while trying to keep one or two cars between them. Sarah made it slightly difficult, weaving in and out of traffic and keeping her speed close to eighty-five miles per hour. The Ford's driver had to work a bit to stay close enough, but that was what Noah wanted.

Following the directions on the GPS, she took the I-495 loop south to North Springfield and then peeled off onto State Route 620. A couple of minutes later she bore left onto 645 for the eight-mile drive into Clifton. The Ford stayed with them.

"Up there," Noah said as he pointed through the windshield. "Looks like some kind of burned-out old building. Turn in there, but make it sudden. I want it to look like we're trying to dig them. As soon as you get off the highway, floor it and try to get around behind the building. I need a few seconds where they can't see us. As soon as we're out of their sight, stop long enough for me and Moose to bail out, then go on a hundred yards and stop again. Turn the car so that you and Neil can get your own guns out the windows. Keep them aimed at the Ford, but do not fire unless you absolutely have to."

In the back seat, Moose lightly backhanded Neil on his shoulder. "Got that? Don't shoot unless you have to!"

"No, really? I couldn't hear the boss just now, thank you for interpreting." Neil withdrew the machine pistol from the computer bag lying on the seat beside him and quickly checked to make sure it was locked and loaded.

Sarah reached into her purse for her Beretta and laid it in her lap. "Okay, hold tight and keep fingers off triggers," she said. "Sharp turn."

She had been cruising the two-lane highway at about sixty, but she had backed off the gas a bit so that her speed had dropped to fifty-five. She hit the brakes suddenly and whipped the wheel to the right, then floored the car once again to take the turn into the parking lot of the abandoned building at almost 50 miles per hour. The car skidded on some loose gravel, but then the all-wheel drive dug in and shot them forward again. A service road seemed to run around the building, so she took it.

Moose, watching through the back window, called out that the Ford had spun out while trying to make the same turn. Sarah had them around the back of the building while the Ford's driver was trying to get the car turned around in the right direction. She slammed on the brakes and skidded to a halt, and Moose and Noah leaped out. As soon as they slammed their doors, she hit the gas again, drove a couple hundred feet more and then slid the car to a stop with the driver's side facing the way they had come. Neil already had his machine pistol out the window and aimed toward where the Ford would appear, and she quickly followed suit with her own pistol.

Moose and Noah had their Glocks in hand, and when the Ford came fishtailing around the corner they both opened fire. Noah's first shot hit the driver in his throat, while Moose took out the left front tire. The car veered left, coming straight toward them, and they had to run to get out of its way before it crashed into the steel pylons of an old water tower.

The two other men in the car were dazed by the impact, but they quickly moved to get out. Both of them came out the passenger side, and the man from the front seat—Pasquale Morabito—fell to the ground. The other stayed on his feet, pistol in hand as he tried to swing around to face Noah and Moose.

"Drop the gun and you might live through this," Noah said, his own gun obviously aimed directly at the man's face. The two of them froze in that position for about five seconds, and then the man carefully stooped down to lay his pistol on the ground. Noah kicked it away.

The man who had fallen was trying to get up while digging for his own gun in its holster. Moose skirted around the first man and put the barrel of his Glock against the fellow's forehead. He had made it to his knees, and carefully raised both hands above his head. Moose took his gun from him and stepped back, motioning for him to stand.

"Where is Nicolaich Andropov?" Noah asked.

The two men glanced at each other, but then both of them shrugged. "Don't know who you mean," Morabito said.

"Are we gonna do this the hard way? Look, gentlemen, let me explain how this is going to work. You are working for Nicolaich Andropov. Your job at the moment, I'm sure, is to keep tabs on me and where I'm at. I want to find Mr. Andropov. You can either tell me where he is, in which case I will let you live, or I can kill one of you right now and leave the other one alive to give Nicolaich a message for me. Which way you wanna do it? Doesn't matter to me."

Morabito started to speak, but the other man cut him off. "Just how long do you think we'd live if we tell you anything you want to know? This Russian, he's crazy, and he's got a hard-on for you like nothing I ever seen. We tell you how to find him, he'll kill us anyway."

Morabito nodded. "He's right, dude. Even if you managed to kill him first, he's got people who would make sure they got us. On the other hand, you leave us alive and we'll tell him whatever message you want. We're only in this for the money, anyway."

Noah looked from one man to the other for a moment. "Money is a really stupid reason to put your life on the line, don't you think? I've never been able to understand the mercenary mind. What does it matter how much money you get promised if you run the risk of dying every single day you're on the job? It's like playing Russian roulette; sooner or later you're bound to lose."

"You run the risk of dying every time you cross the street," Morabito said. "At least if you're making big money, you can live pretty good until the odds catch up with you. Hell, you ain't no different than we are. I know who you are, I know what you do; you get paid to kill people. Isn't that being a mercenary?"

"Do you think I give a shit what you think of me?" Noah asked him. "I only need one of you to deliver my message, so my question still remains the same. Tell me where to find Nicolaich and I let you walk away from here. You can disappear, go somewhere he'll never find you. Don't tell me and one of you dies today. You have thirty seconds to decide."

The two men stared at each other for several seconds, and then the other man turned to Noah. "Here's the problem," he said. "In our business, you never talk—and if you do, you make sure there's nobody left who can snitch on you for doing it. You want to know where the Russian is?" He hooked a thumb at Morabito. "You kill this piece of crap and I'll tell you."

Morabito's eyes went wide as he looked at his companion, and then even wider when he saw Noah's gun swing toward his face. It was the last thing he ever saw, because both of his eyes imploded as the hollow-point slug passed between them and blew out the back of his head.

The gun instantly went back to the other man. "Done," Noah said. "Where is Nicolaich?"

The man looked down at the corpse beside him for a second or two, then looked up at Noah. "I can't give you his exact location because he keeps it secret, only a few people know it, but I can tell you how to find him tomorrow. He's got this habit, see? Every Wednesday, dead on 11 o'clock in the morning, he calls his daughter in Russia so he can talk to his grandson. The kid's only like seven or eight, and the old man is crazy about him. Doesn't matter where he is or what he's doing, he'll drop it to make that call."

Noah glanced at Moose. "Get Neil over here," he said. Moose nodded and jogged toward the car as Noah turned back to his informant. "What's your name?"

"Tom Bridger," the man said. "I don't know the daughter's number, but I'm pretty sure you can get it. He always talks to the kid for half an hour, should give you plenty of time to run a trace and get a location, right?"

Sarah drove the car closer while Moose jogged back to Noah, and Neil slid out of the backseat when they got there. He kept his machine pistol pointed at Bridger as he approached, and avoided looking down at the corpse. "Yeah, Boss?"

"I just found out that Nicolaich calls his daughter in Russia every Wednesday morning. How hard would it be for you to track down her number and trace the call back to Nicolaich when he makes it?"

Neil snorted. "I'm sure we can get her number from NSA," he said. "There's a half-dozen ways I can tap her line, then when he calls it I just start tracing back. The problem could be if he uses a lot of reroutes. If it takes too long to get back to his originating phone, he'll be off the line before I get a location."

"Like I said," Bridger put in, "he always talks to the kid for at least a half hour."

Neil shrugged. "Half an hour should be plenty, but it still boils down to how many different forwarding numbers he runs it through. I'd say the odds are pretty good. To stay hidden in a half-hour phone call, he'd have to bounce the call dozens of times. It's not like you see in the movies, where you have to keep somebody talking for so many minutes to trace a call. Nowadays it's pretty much instantaneous, but each time the call is forwarded, you have to punch in another whole trace. Figure each one takes maybe twenty seconds to set up, he'd have to bounce through ninety different phones to make sure I couldn't track him back to the phone he's using. If it's a landline, the phone company will have an address for it that I can hack, and a cell phone will give me its GPS location." He grinned. "I think we can do this, Boss."

Noah nodded thoughtfully, then looked back at Bridger. "Of course, that's assuming you're telling me the truth. Then the only problem that remains is how to be sure you don't warn him that I'm going to be tracing that call."

Bridger smiled. "I look stupid to you? If I go back to him now, after these guys are dead, he's gonna naturally figure I gave up something and put a bullet in my head. The only hope I've got of staying alive now is to disappear as fast as I can. You ain't gotta worry about me saying anything."

"I know," Noah said as he squeezed the trigger. The bullet took Bridger's left eye, and most of the left side of his head seemed to explode out the back. His body stood for almost three seconds more before it fell.

"Jesus!" Neil said, his eyes wide and his face pale. "Jesus, Boss! He told you what you wanted to know! You said you wouldn't kill him if he told you what you wanted to know!"

"Chill out, Neil," Moose said. "The guy would probably have gone straight back to Nicolaich, and even if he tried to run, Nicolaich would catch him before he could get out of town. Noah did exactly what he had to do."

"Get into the car," Noah said. "Let's get back to the hotel and get you started on whatever you have to do to catch and trace that call. If Bridger was telling the truth, we've got one possible shot at getting Nicolaich before he can get Molly or me. We can't afford to miss the chance, even if it's just a long shot."

"Yeah, but…"

"In the car, Neil, now," Noah said, then he turned to Moose. "We want this to look like a firefight." He picked up Morabito's gun and forced it into the dead man's hand. He put Morabito's finger on the trigger, then fired the entire clip into the air as Moose did the same with Bridger's pistol.

They got into the car, where Neil was leaning against the window he had raised and crying quietly. Noah turned his head around to look at the boy, but Sarah reached up and put a hand to his cheek, forcing him to look forward again. As he did so, he noticed that her own face was very pale.

SIXTEEN

Neil was quiet all the way back to the hotel and went straight to his room when they got there. Noah started to follow him but Moose caught his arm.

"First time he ever saw somebody get killed," Moose said quietly, since they were standing in the hallway. "Let me handle him, okay, Boss?"

Noah started to say something but Sarah took hold of his hand. "Come on, Babe," she said. "I'm pretty shook up myself. Neil and I aren't normally involved in those parts of the missions. Knowing that you kill people and actually seeing you do it are two different things, believe me. He'll be okay, he's just got to get his head wrapped around it."

"He has to," Noah said as he let her lead them into their room. "He's got to run the phone tap tomorrow, and he needs to get on it today."

Sarah closed the door and then turned to face Noah. She just looked at him for a moment, then reached up to put her arms around his neck. She pulled him close and laid her head on his chest.

It took Noah a couple of minutes to realize that she was crying, as well. He tried to look down at her face without disturbing her but it wasn't possible, so he hooked a finger under her chin and tipped her face up. "I understand," he said. "I've seen other people, when they first witness a violent death. We had a couple of guys in the Army just couldn't cope with it, they ended up sending them home not long after the first time they had to kill anyone. The thing is, it's not your first time. You saw me killing Nicolaich's men when I got you out of the club in Russia."

She barked out something that was a combination of laugh and sob. "I know you won't get this, but I wasn't really paying a lot of attention to who you were shooting at the time. I was too busy ducking and praying I was going to get out of it alive. All I remember about that day is running and then watching you damn near bleed to death. Can't say I really recall anybody getting shot, at least not other than just academically, you know, like I know it happened even if I can't remember a specific instance. I mean, I know you shot people, and Moose did, too. That doesn't mean I saw it happen."

Noah looked into her eyes. "I understand. Is there anything I can do for you?"

She leaned her head forward until her forehead was against his breastbone. "Right at the moment, probably the best thing you could do for me is take me to bed. Can we spare the time?"

Noah grabbed her butt and lifted as she wrapped her arms and legs around him, then carried her to the bed. "We'll make time."

* * * * *

It was an hour later when Noah's phone rang, and he picked it up to see that it was Moose calling. "Hello?"

"I thought you'd want to know that Neil is okay," Moose said. "He walked in here and sat down at his computer and started playing some black ops game, but after a while he shut it down and we talked. He'll be fine; he's in the head right at the moment. He's got the Andropov girl's phone number all set up for tomorrow, by the way."

"Good. If this pans out, we might be able to bring this to an end pretty quickly."

"Yep. And, hey, while I got you on the phone, has anybody but me paid attention to the fact that we skipped lunch? My stomach is starting to think somebody cut my throat."

Noah glanced at Sarah, who was cuddled up against him with her head on his shoulder. "Getting hungry?"

She made a face that indicated indifference. "I could eat, but I'm not starving."

"Okay, it's…" He pulled his phone away from his ear and looked at the time display. "It's almost three. Give us half an hour and we'll go find us a late lunch."

"Okay, Boss."

Noah put down the phone and looked at Sarah's face again. "I need a quick shower," he said, and then he kissed her forehead as he rolled up out of the bed.

"Me, too," Sarah said. She tossed off the covers and made it into the bathroom before he did, leaving the door open as an invitation to him to follow.

They had just finished dressing when a tap on their door told them Moose and Neil were ready to go. Noah slipped his holstered Glock onto the back of his belt and covered it with the light gray jacket he often wore, as Sarah picked up her purse. He opened the door and they stepped out together, then the four of them rode down the elevator and walked out to the car.

As soon as they got into the car, Neil laid his computer on the seat and then reached up to tap Noah on the shoulder. "Sorry about that, Boss," he said. "Guess I freaked out a bit."

"No sweat," Noah said. "Let's forget about it, okay?"

"Okay," Neil said, sounding relieved. "Listen, I got Marina Andropov's phone number from the NSA database and got it set up with a 'trap and tap' program. My computer is set up to record and trace any call that goes to that number for the next twenty-four hours, automatically. I figured I'd give it that long, just in case he was either early or late."

"Good job. Now we just hope Bridger was telling the truth. For right now, let's just all keep an eye out for tails." He reached into a pocket and took out his phone, then dialed Molly's number. She answered on the second ring.

"How's it going out there, Mr. Spock?" she asked. "Can I stop worrying yet?"

"Not just yet," Noah said, "but we may have picked up a lead that will help us get to that point. Unfortunately, we won't know until tomorrow sometime, so you stay close to your shadows."

"That's easy," Molly said. "They won't let me out of their sight. One of my supervisors came running into my office a couple hours ago to ask a question, and Ms. Sanchez had him flat on his back with a gun pointed at his head so fast I never got the chance to tell her he was okay. The poor guy is in his 60s, I think he almost had a heart attack."

"Good, that means she's doing her job. Have them take you straight home after work, no stops and no social calls. They'll switch out for the second shift about then, and between your bodyguards and the security around your place, you should be okay tonight."

"Yeah, Lassiter took it upon himself to notify Blackstone of a possible threat on me, and they called a while ago to tell me they're stepping up their patrols tonight. I'll have two of yours inside the house, four of theirs outside and three cars circling the block all night long."

"Like I said, they're doing their jobs. I'll be in touch later, but you can call me if you need to."

"I suspect I'll be fine," Molly said. "Hey, by the way, I'm just curious—are the guys on the night shift any better looking than Lassiter? And maybe single?"

"Probably not, on both counts. Keep it together, Molly, you can't afford any distractions tonight."

"I know, I know, but you can't blame a girl for hoping, right? Okay, I'll talk to you later."

As Noah put the phone back into his pocket, Sarah looked over at him. "As far as I can tell, no one is tailing us. Anybody got a preference on where we go to eat? There's a smorgasbord up here on the left."

"Smorgasbord!" Neil yelled from the back seat. "All-you-can-eat! That's perfect, let's go there."

"I second that motion," Moose said. "It's been way too long since breakfast."

Sarah surprised herself by laughing at them, but moved into the left lane so that she could make the turn into the parking lot. "It blows my mind how we can be so focused and violent, and then be joking and laughing just a couple of hours later. I wonder if it's a personality trait that they looked for when they were recruiting us."

"Yeah," Neil said, "they look for the genetic markers of sociopathic insanity. If you're crazy enough, they offer you a job."

Noah suddenly snapped his fingers. "Then, that explains how I got here, right?"

Sarah stopped the car in a parking space and stared at him. Moose and Neil both leaned forward into the space between the bucket seats, their own eyes locked on his face.

It was Sarah who finally broke the silence. "Babe," she said, "we all understand that you don't really have much of a grasp on humor, so when you try to make a joke, all it does is come off as really disturbing."

Noah looked from one to the other, blankly. "Does it really? I used to do it all the time, Molly said it would help me seem normal."

"I can see that," Neil said, "but let me ask you a question. Did Molly ever laugh at your jokes? If nobody else was around, I mean?"

Noah's eyebrows came down just a bit. "Now that you mention it, I don't think she did."

Neil was nodding his head. "That's because she knew you the way we do. We're fully aware that you don't have, as she put it, certain parts of the normal human programming. We're used to you just being yourself around us, so when you try to act 'normal,' all it does is send a chill down our spines. Please don't do that anymore, not when you're just with us."

The eyebrows popped back upward, and Noah got out of the car without response. The rest of them followed and they walked into the restaurant.

The next two hours were occupied with eating. Sarah surprised herself again by eating more than she had expected, but all three of the men made multiple trips through the line. Yankee pot roast, fried chicken, pork chops, beef ribs and several different varieties of fish made it onto their plates, along with generous helpings of mashed potatoes and gravy, green beans and sweet corn on the cob, and all of them finished up with ice cream, brownies and banana pudding.

There was no talk of missions or enemies, because the place was just too well packed. Noah had cued the rest of them to use their cover names by looking at Sarah and asking, "Rosie, baby, would you get me some iced tea, please?" From that moment on, they referred to each other as Wyatt, Rosie, Jimmy and Lenny.

They were finishing up dessert when Noah's phone rang. The caller ID said the call was coming from Brigadoon, so Noah answered instantly. "Yes, Sir, this is Wyatt," he said.

Parker chuckled. "Well, hello Wyatt," he said. "Doc Holliday, here. I thought you might like an update on Annie Oakley."

"Yes, Sir, I sure would. How's she doing?"

"Meaner than a striped-ass snake! The doctors say the swelling in her brain has gone down, and she's regaining most of what she lost. I can tell you that her tongue is definitely back to normal, because she's been lashing me with it for the last two hours. Her abdominal surgery went through without a hitch, and the bullet in her leg didn't do a whole lot of damage, so those aren't much of a concern, right now. They're going to keep her a few more days for observation, but she'll probably be back in her office within a week."

"Tell her we're all glad to hear it, Sir. How about Mr. J?"

"He's at home, now. I did find out that he lost about a third of his left lung, but he's in good enough shape in general that it shouldn't affect him too much, according to the doctors. He's been ordered to stay off work for at least a month, possibly longer."

"Again, good news. Things are going okay out here. I'll call in a report later today, if that's okay."

"Yes, as soon as you can. I'm curious about a report we got of three known mercenaries who seem to have met an untimely end out your way."

"You know my business motto, Sir, eliminate the competition."

"I thought that might be how it was. Call me later with more details."

"Yes…" Noah didn't get any further because the line went dead. Everyone else had finished up while he was talking—even Neil, who literally scraped the minute bits of banana pudding from the bowl—so they got up and left.

As soon as they were in the car, Noah filled them in on Allison and Jefferson. All three of the others expressed delight that their bosses were doing so well, and then Noah called Doc Parker back.

"Report, Camelot," the old man said.

"Yes, Sir," Noah replied. "Three of Nicolaich's men followed us this morning after we left Molly's office. I decided it was time to send Nicolaich a message of my own, so we allowed them to trail us out into the countryside. I spotted an abandoned industrial building and instructed Sarah to pull in suddenly and drive behind it. Moose and I jumped out of the car and waited for our shadows to appear, and I took out the driver first. The car crashed and the other two climbed out. By the time they got to their feet we were able to disarm. One was Pasquale Morabito, who refused to tell me anything, and the other was a man named Tom Bridger. Bridger offered to reveal Nicolaich's location if I would kill Morabito, so I did. Afterward, Bridger admitted that he didn't know where to find Nicolaich, but said that Nicolaich calls his daughter every Wednesday at precisely 11 local time. Neil said that he could trace the call to get a location, and I killed Bridger to ensure that he could not warn Nicolaich."

"Excellent work. Of course, I'm certain you considered the possibility that this is part of Andropov's plan, that he may have deliberately planted this Bridger with such a suggestion. He's quite capable of sacrificing his own pawns for a chance to capture a king."

"Yes, Sir, I think that's quite possible. Bridger may have been instructed to offer the information if confronted, and to sacrifice Morabito to make it more believable. If that's the case, Nicolaich will undoubtedly be gone by the time we arrive, with snipers in place to try to take us out."

"Exactly. When I saw the report come in about the three casualties, I suspected that it might have included information that could lead you into a trap. I can't risk losing you right now, so I've taken the liberty of requesting a Delta Force squadron to be placed under your command. They're being transported to you in a C-

130, and you should hear from their commanding officer within the next three hours. Your orders are to separate them into response teams and deploy them around the area. That way, at least one of them should be within a reasonable distance if you get a location on Andropov. Let them handle the takedown, Camelot. Stress to them that there is no need to take Andropov alive. His corpse will suffice and can be positively identified. We obtained samples of his DNA from the broken glass Ms. Child used to put out his eye. It seems our man in Moscow has some connections with the police, there, and was able to get it after your confrontation with him in the bar."

"Yes, Sir," Noah said. "Under the circumstances, that's a logical decision. May I request permission to join the active engagement when it begins?"

"Camelot, we're talking about Delta Force. These guys are the equivalent of SEAL Team Six, the active engagement will probably be over before you can get there, but permission granted anyway. Just don't get yourself killed in the process."

The phone went dead and Noah relayed the instructions to the rest of the team.

"Okay, that just sucks," Neil said. "I know I got shook up when you killed that guy earlier, but I was looking forward to watching you take out Nicolaich. Attacking Neverland was a mistake, and he needs to pay for it."

"He will," Noah said, and the coldness in his voice was deeper than usual. "It's well after five. Let's take a ride down by Molly's place and see if we can pick up another shadow."

"You got it," Sarah said as she backed the car out and pointed it in the right direction. "Um—is this going to be like the last time?"

"I'm not sure," Noah said. "Depends on how they react. Odds on, they already know what happened to the last batch. I doubt they'll be so easy to draw into any kind of a trap."

"What's to keep them from just opening fire on us?" Neil asked. "I understand this is a supercar, but I don't think it's bulletproof."

"It probably isn't," Noah said, "but I don't think that's something we have to worry about. Nicolaich isn't likely to want someone else taking me down. Whatever he's up to, he simply wants to know where I am and what I'm doing."

"Wait a minute," Sarah said. "I thought we were certain he was still going after Molly."

"He almost certainly is, but with the security we've got on her right now, it would be damned hard to get to her. It isn't likely he'll try it tonight; he'll want to observe the heightened security for at least a couple of days, first. On the other hand, he's probably getting frustrated that we keep losing his tails. He'll have somebody there just to watch and see if I show up. We don't want to disappoint them, now, do we?"

SEVENTEEN

As Noah had predicted, a white Ford Crown Victoria was parked less than a block from the entrance to Molly's subdivision. Sarah had to drive past it as they approached the entrance and Noah looked into the car as they did so, smiled and waved at the four men inside and then watched in the visor mirror as the car pulled out behind them.

"Amazing," Neil said. "They seem to think it's a good idea to stay back a ways. Wonder what gave them that idea?"

"I'm sure Nicolaich is monitoring police radio traffic," Noah said. "Somebody would have found the results of our earlier handiwork by now, so they've undoubtedly been told to do what they can to stay out of range. All they're supposed to do is keep us in sight and try to find out where we're staying."

"Oh, that's peachy. What do you say we disappoint them on that part, can we do that?"

"I second that motion," Sarah put in.

"Don't worry, I have no intention of letting them trace us back to the hotel. With any luck, we can stay completely off their radar until after Nicolaich makes his call tomorrow. If the situation is unresolved tomorrow afternoon, we'll need to find a new base of operations. There are only so many hotels in the area; sooner or later, Nicolaich would find us."

"Yeah, I was thinking about that when we were back at the hotel," Neil said. "I looked around online to see if there might be a better place and found a couple of good prospects. There's an extremely private estate sitting in the middle of forty acres on the Potomac River that caught my eye, and it's less than thirty minutes from DC. No staff, and all it would take to rent it for anywhere from a week to a year is a phone call."

"Good, we'll keep it in mind. Hopefully these Delta Force operators can bring this to a conclusion tomorrow so that it isn't an issue. If not, we'll snatch that up."

They spent the next two hours just riding around the Metroplex, keeping their followers occupied. When Sarah glanced down at the gas gauge and saw that it was getting low, she looked over at Noah.

"We're gonna need gas," she said. "Want me to shake them now?"

Noah was quiet for several seconds, then shook his head. "No. Everyone get weapons ready, just in case they decide to make a move. Go ahead and hit the next gas station. You'll all stay in the car, and I'll get out to pump the gas."

Sarah swallowed hard, but she pulled into the next gas station as she was told and parked beside the pumps. The Crown Victoria drove on past the gas station, but then pulled over and stopped less than half a block ahead.

"Keep the weapons ready, but it looks like we don't have a problem," Noah said as he got out of the car. He walked around to the driver's side and inserted a credit card into the pump, then removed the nozzle and began filling the tank. As the gas flowed in, he stood there and watched the white car.

The occupants were apparently watching in the mirrors, because no one turned around to look at him. He waved in their direction and the sudden bobbing of heads inside confirmed that they were keeping an eye on him, even though they carefully avoided looking directly back in his direction.

When the pump clicked off, he put it back and secured the gas cap, then walked around to get back into the car. As they pulled away, the Ford fell in behind them once again.

"Yep!" Neil said. "They know what happened to the last guys, they're not going to get close enough to let us get a shot at them, are they?"

"Us?" Moose asked. "As I recall, Noah and I were the only ones who did any shooting."

Neil spun his head toward Moose and stuck out his tongue. "I would have pulled the trigger, if you guys didn't have it already under control. Sarah and I were only there as backups, remember? Trust me, if I have to, I'll pull that trigger!"

"Don't let him get your goat, Neil," Sarah said. "I swear, you two really must be brothers, the way you bicker."

Moose grinned. "Hey, you two are always treating him with kid gloves. Somebody has to stay on his ass, might as well be me."

Noah sat quietly in his seat, occasionally raising his eyes to look at the Ford in the visor mirror. His analytical mind, however, was making note of the fact that his team had so well developed into a close and loyal unit that they were all comfortable picking on each other.

His phone rang as he was having these thoughts. "Hello?"

"Camelot?"

"Yes, go ahead," Noah said.

"Sir, this is Captain Oliver Hayes with Delta Force Squadron A. I have orders to report to you for assignment."

"Yes, Captain. Where are you now?"

"Sir, we just landed at Joint Base Andrews, but we are currently being loaded into a pair of buses that will take us out to a Joint Special Operations Command facility near Dulles. If you like, we can meet there. Is your phone secure?"

"Yes," Noah said. "Can you text me the GPS coordinates?"

"Hell, I'll just send you the address. The place looks like an old motel, but you'll need a pass code to get past the guard shack. I'll send you that, as well. We should be there in just about an hour, look forward to seeing you then."

"That sounds good, Captain," Noah said. "We'll meet you there."

He ended the call, but his phone buzzed only a moment later with the address and pass phrase that would gain them entrance. Noah tapped the address and his phone's GPS immediately began giving directions. It would take them slightly over half an hour to arrive, but first they had to lose the Crown Victoria that was following.

"Okay, Babe, it's time to shake our tail."

Sarah grinned, then rolled down her window and stuck her hand out into the air. "Just waving bye-bye," she said, then pulled her hand back in and powered up the window. A moment later she made a hard left turn and gave the turbocharged Hemi engine its head.

The car shot forward as if it had a JATO rocket strapped to its tail, and the Crown Victoria was hopelessly left behind within three blocks. Sarah weaved around a semi truck and then tapped a button to change the silver car to yellow just before braking hard in order to take an on-ramp for I-495. Noah watched in the visor mirror as the Crown Victoria sailed past the ramp in a vain attempt to catch up to the elusive silver Chrysler.

Sarah dropped her speed to eighty-five miles per hour, keeping up with the traffic on the loop highway. They would have to make their way around most of the Alexandria/Annandale area to get to I-66 for the rest of the trip to their destination.

"That was awfully easy," Neil said. "Would you expect them to be better at following someone?"

"Not really," Sarah said. "They were hanging back so far that it was easy to put some distance between us. They were trying to keep their eyes on a silver car more than two blocks ahead, they never noticed a yellow one going up the on-ramp. If I'd had this car back when I was running blocker for my dad, we never would've gotten busted."

Neil and Moose looked at each other, and Moose shrugged. "What's that mean, running blocker?" Neil asked.

Sarah laughed. "Unless it was absolutely necessary, Dad didn't want me actually stealing a car myself. Instead, he'd give me something fast and flashy and I'd use it to keep the cops off his ass. I'd get in front of them and slow down, weave around so they couldn't pass me, and he'd get away with whatever car he had just snatched. As soon as he was out of sight, I'd shake the cops the same way we just shook those idiots." She twisted her face into an irritating grimace. "That's how I got caught and ended up at E & E. We tried it one time too many in San Francisco and the cops caught on. I was driving a new Mustang and they managed to get one ahead of me. He T-boned me in the passenger side, but my dad saw it in the rearview mirror and came back to see if I was okay. He was surrounded by the time he got out of the car and they tased him, then stuffed him in a squad car and took him to jail while they were still waiting for an ambulance for me. I woke up the next day with tubes sticking out of me and my leg in a cast, and Allison was sitting there looking at me. She told me that if I would join E & E, she would see to it that my dad didn't do any time and would be offered a big-money job using his skills to help the FBI fight interstate auto theft. I agreed, and as far as my dad knows, I died in that wreck." A single tear made its way down her cheek. "Anyway, if I'd had this? They could have kissed my ass!"

All three of the men were silent for a moment, but then Neil reached up and patted her shoulder. "I hope you won't take this the wrong way," he said, "but I'm pretty glad you did get caught. Otherwise, we wouldn't have you to make sure we get where we're going in one piece. I don't think anybody could outdrive you."

Sarah smiled again. "Mario Andretti, maybe, but I think he's dead. Isn't he dead?"

"Just a minute, I'll tell you—nope, he's not dead, he's just old."

It was almost seven thirty when Sarah pulled up to the gatehouse at the JSOC Compound, and two Marines carrying M4 rifles stepped out and flanked the car. Noah rolled down his window.

"I'm here to meet Squadron A. Pass code is 14 Alpha 5-9 Zulu Charlie."

"Your name, Sir?" the guard asked.

"The name is Camelot," Noah said.

"Yes, Sir, you're approved for entry. Please follow the blue stars on the roadway, they'll take you directly to the TOC. There's a Colonel Abrams there waiting for you now."

The guards stepped away and the large steel gate slid open. Sarah put the car in gear and moved forward, keeping it down to the fifteen-mile-per-hour speed limit that was posted.

There were red, white and blue stars on the road, each apparently leading to a different part of the compound. Sarah followed the blue stars onto a curving road, and fifteen minutes later they arrived at a large concrete building. Another gate opened as they approached, and a soldier in fatigues directed them to a parking area.

"Neil," Noah said, "bring your computer."

As they got out of the car, a woman in an army uniform stepped out of the building to greet them. "You must be Camelot," she said to Noah. "I'm Colonel Jennifer Abrams. I don't know who you are and I don't think I want to know, but JSOC says I am to extend you every courtesy and assistance possible."

Noah stuck out a hand and the Colonel shook it firmly. "Good to meet you, Colonel. For now, you can call me Wyatt. These folks with me are Rosemary, Jimmy and Lenny. I imagine we've arrived a little before Captain Hayes, am I right?"

"I'm afraid so. I haven't been briefed on what this is about, so I'm not going to ask any questions. However, I've got to tell you, I get a little concerned when Delta Force gets called into town. My understanding is that they are to answer to you and you alone for the duration of whatever operation you're running."

"Yes, that's my understanding as well. Since you haven't been briefed, I'm going to assume that I'm not supposed to tell you all the details, but I can hopefully relieve your nerves a little bit. This is a fairly simple operation with the goal of catching a single individual. I don't believe that anyone outside the operation is in any danger, if that helps."

Colonel Abrams smiled. "It actually does," she said. "Around here, our biggest fear is some sort of mass destruction event. All of my kids live around here and work in DC, so when I heard Delta was coming in, it was all I could do not to panic." She suddenly lost focus and put a hand to her left ear, where Noah could see an ear bud with a curling wire going down into the collar of her jacket. "Roger that," she said. She looked back up at Noah. "The buses just came through the gate. We've got a briefing room all set up for you inside, if you care to follow me." She turned without another word and led them into the large structure.

Colonel Abrams showed them into what almost looked like an empty warehouse. There were several dozen chairs already set up, and a speaker's podium with a microphone at the front of the room. A table on the side held several large coffee urns along with many boxes of doughnuts. Neil let out a yelp of excitement and headed for the table, with Moose right behind him.

Noah turned to Sarah. "Rosie, would you get me a cup of coffee and one of those doughnuts? I'd like to speak to the Colonel for just a moment."

Sarah blinked and went to do as she was told. Noah turned back to Colonel Abrams.

"Colonel, I appreciate your assistance on this. I've never worked with Delta Force before. Is there anything you can think of I need to know, before they get here?"

The Colonel smiled at him. "I'll give you the same advice that was given to me the first time I had to deal with them. These men are among the best of the best, but they are trained to follow orders. The only thing they ask is that whoever is giving those orders knows what he's doing. Something about you tells me they don't have to worry about it, this time. You've got an Army bearing about you."

"Yes, Ma'am," Noah said, "but I'm afraid my military record is classified."

Colonel Abrams nodded sagely. "You know, it's funny," she said. "You remind me of a young sergeant who was all over the news about eight months ago. He had the same blond hair and blue eyes as you, but your nose and chin are different." She looked into his eyes for a moment, but then dropped her eyes to the ground. "As Forrest Gump might say, that's all I've got to say about that."

EIGHTEEN

Noah kept his face straight and said nothing as Sarah slowly approached him with two cups of coffee and a couple of doughnuts on a napkin. It was taking both hands to carry it all and the look on her face told him the coffee was very hot. He met her partway and took one of the cups from her, then relieved her of a doughnut. He had just finished eating it when two buses pulled up outside and Colonel Abrams led the seventy men of Squadron A into the building.

A man with longish brown hair and beard looked at Noah and raised his eyebrows. "Camelot? I'm Captain Hayes."

Noah extended a hand. "I'm Camelot, but you can call me Wyatt. They set us up with coffee and doughnuts. If you and your men want to help yourselves and then settle in, we can begin the briefing."

"Yes, Sir," Hayes said. He turned toward the table with the refreshments, where his men were already helping themselves. "All right, you mooks, get the goodies and take a chair. Five minutes, snap it up."

It actually took almost 10 minutes, but finally everyone was sitting down and looking at Noah. Neil had found a digital projector and connected his computer to it, and Colonel Abrams had produced a table and chair for him. Once everyone was seated, she and the soldiers who had set up the room walked out the door, closing it behind them.

Noah nodded to Neil, and the screen on the wall behind him suddenly lit up with a photograph of Nicolaich Andropov. The photo was one that the CIA had managed to get of him a month earlier, showing him with an eye patch and a jagged scar on his left cheek.

"The man on the screen behind me is Nicolaich Andropov, a former director of wet work for the SVR in Russia. For the past several years, he used his position to allow him to gather incredible amounts of information, a lot of which was designed to force political figures to cooperate with him at his discretion. He was behind an attempt four months ago to force the government of Mauritania to enter into an alliance they didn't want. To facilitate that plan, he arranged for the abduction of the daughter of the president of that country. My team was sent in to find the girl and recover her, which we did. In the course of doing so, I killed Vasily Andropov, Nicolaich's youngest son. Nicolaich then used his SVR forces, in violation of Russian law, to attempt to exact revenge against me. He abducted one of my team in an attempt to draw me into a trap, but I was able to recover her and we escaped with our lives. Unfortunately, Nicolaich also survived."

Noah stepped out from behind the podium and leaned on it with his elbow. "Several days ago, a team of mercenaries attacked a small town in Colorado. Their aim was to inflict damage on the organization that I work for, as part of yet another plan of Andropov's to seek his revenge against me. Our investigation has led us here, where he had apparently been planning to either abduct or murder one of my childhood friends. He is currently running a team of hired guns who seem to be doing little more than surveillance. They had been watching my old friend, but I let them see that I was in town and their efforts seem to be more focused on myself, now. My team and I cornered three of them earlier today and learned that Nicolaich will be making an international phone call to Russia at just about 11 tomorrow morning.

"My intelligence officer," he said, pointing at Neil, "is prepared to trace that call and determine the location from which it was made. My plan is to divide you into response teams that can be dispersed around the metro area, so that at least one team can hopefully arrive at that location before Nicolaich can get away."

He stood there for a moment, just looking over the men in front of him. "It is absolutely imperative," he said at last, "that Nicolaich Andropov does not escape. This man is a master of manipulation; if you get the shot, take it. Any attempt to take him alive will only increase the possibility that he will escape, and we cannot allow that."

The men were silent, staring at the photo displayed on the screen. Each of them, Noah knew, was committing every detail of Andropov's face to memory.

"As I mentioned earlier, Nicolaich has a team of mercenaries working with him. It is highly unlikely that you will find him alone, and it is possible that he may even have innocent civilians in the area, potential hostages. I expect you to make every reasonable attempt to avoid or minimalize collateral damage, but the elimination of Nicolaich Andropov must take precedence over anything else. This man has set himself up as a power and weapons broker, and he is in possession of enough extortable knowledge to topple governments or start wars. He presents an even greater danger to the world than Osama bin Laden ever was, and absolutely must be eliminated if at all possible, even if it means endangering civilians. Any questions?"

Captain Hayes, sitting in the front row, stood up. "Sir, how many teams do you want to set up? My men can operate well in three-, five- or seven-man teams."

"Five-man teams would probably be ideal," Noah replied. He looked at Neil and nodded, and a Google map of the area appeared on the screen. "We need to position five teams in DC itself, two in Alexandria, two more in Arlington and we'll space the others out around the perimeter of the area. I'll need a line of communications through you, Captain, to each team. As soon as we have a location, the nearest teams will immediately move to converge on it, and the rest can move in to assist as possible."

"Yes, Sir. As soon as you're done with us, we'll move to strategy planning and start getting this set up. You said this call is scheduled for 11 AM?"

"That's correct."

"Then we'll bunk down here tonight, and I'll have the teams in place by six. This facility has a number of vehicles, and we brought our weapons with us. It won't be any problem to have them on station by six AM. As for communications, I'll give you a special secure cell number that you can send a text message to. That message will go to every team at the same instant. If you send a street address or GPS coordinates, their phones will instantly tell them how far they are from that location and offer them directions. With the spacing you seem to have in mind, there should be two or more teams within only a few minutes of any spot within that region. The closest team will take lead, and the others will coordinate with them." He handed Noah a small handheld radio receiver. "This is set to our secure channel, it will let you listen in when things start happening."

Noah nodded. "That's excellent," he said. "It sounds like you guys have done this sort of thing before."

Captain Hayes smiled. "On a couple of occasions," he said. "This is the kind of thing we live for, Sir. It's why we exist."

"One more thing," Noah said. "I hope not to see any of your men on the after-action casualty reports, but Nicolaich is one of the most dangerous men alive. He has absolutely no morals and no compunctions against using innocent civilians as pawns or distractions. This is not a time for heroism, I'm afraid. If you expose yourselves, you will be dead. You must understand that it's necessary to do whatever it takes to eliminate this man, up to and including the destruction of whatever building he's in."

Captain Hayes nodded his understanding. "Yes, Sir, we get it. I can assure you that you've got the right people for the job."

"Very good, then, Captain," Noah said. "I'll turn this over to you, then."

Hayes turned to face his men and barked out fourteen names, instantly splitting the group into the teams they would be operating in. Two of them grabbed a folding table that was leaning against the wall and set it up, while Hayes produced a large map of the area. The men he had named gathered around the table as Hayes pointed out coordinates on the map, giving each team leader his position. As each man understood where he was to wait with his team for the word on Andropov's location, he walked away and began talking with the four who would accompany him. It seemed that everyone had a cell phone in his hand, and they were all pressing buttons frantically with their thumbs, synchronizing the communication devices to one another.

Noah was still standing by the podium when Sarah appeared at his side. "Shouldn't you be over there with the captain?"

Noah shook his head. "No, he knows what he's doing. This is his end of the operation, ours is just to let them know where to go."

Moose, who had been sitting beside the doughnuts, joined them a moment later. "These guys seem like they know their shit," he said, "but I'd feel a little better if they were SEAL Team Six."

Noah glanced at him. "Delta Force is their sister organization. Both of them get the best commando training in the world."

"Ignore him, Boss," Neil said. "He's just prejudiced against these Army guys cause he flunked out of SEAL school."

Moose playfully smacked Neil in the back of the head. "I did not flunk out," he said. "I got fed up with the crap and got myself kicked out! There's a difference!"

"Enough," Noah said. "I need these men to respect my orders, so act professional." He walked over to where Captain Hayes was speaking with four men of his own. "Captain, is there any way I can be of assistance to you?"

Hayes looked up at him with a smile. "You already have," he said. "We've been sitting on our thumbs for the last three months, just wishing for a mission. We train every day, but sometimes the training gets old. Guys like us, we live for the real thing. As far as right now, Sir, I think we've got a grasp on the situation. Colonel Abrams will assign us some nice civilian-looking vehicles that we can stage in, so I think we got it covered." He took out his phone and began punching buttons. "I'm texting you the broadcast number now. When you get a location, send it as a text message on that number and we'll all get it at once."

"I will," Noah said, as his phone buzzed in his pocket. "I'm going to take my team back to our base of operations. You've got my number if you need me for anything."

"Yes, Sir," Hayes said. "If anything comes up, I'll be in touch. If not, we'll just wait to hear from you tomorrow."

Noah shook his hand once more, then turned and gathered his team by eye. They walked out the door together and found Colonel Abrams standing just outside the building entrance.

"Everything taken care of?" she asked.

"It is," Noah said. "Captain Hayes has everything under control, I think. I'm taking my team back to our base of operations so that we can relax for a bit and get ready for the action that will take place tomorrow, but I wanted to thank you for your assistance."

The Colonel cocked her head to one side and gave him a half smile. "I suspect that I could make an educated guess about you, but I'm going to fight off that temptation. The only thing I'm sure of at this moment is that whatever you're doing has to do with protecting our country. I'll be glad to give you any kind of assistance I can, at any time."

She suddenly snapped a perfect salute at him, and Noah returned it automatically. When he dropped his hand, he extended it and shook her, and then walked toward the car without another word.

"Back to the hotel?" Sarah asked.

"Yeah," Noah said. "Neil can go over the setup for tomorrow and then we can try to relax for a while tonight. Take a roundabout way getting back there; we don't want to pick up any more shadows today if we can avoid it."

Sarah nodded and put the car in gear. She followed the blue stars back to the gate and the guards waved as they passed through it. When she got to the interstate, however, she didn't bother to get on but continued straight until she came to a large intersection.

The ride back to the hotel took slightly over an hour, but there was no sign of any surveillance by the time they got there. A quick pass through the parking lot didn't reveal any sign of clandestine observation so they parked and headed up to their rooms. Moose and Neil followed Noah and Sarah into their room, and Neil set up his computer on the table.

"Just on the off chance that anything were to happen to me," he said to Noah, "I want you to see how this works. I've created a bot that will handle the whole trace, and it will generate a report as soon as it begs the location of the originating phone. That report will cause this little red star to flash, so if for any reason I'm not here to read for you, all you need to do is touch that icon to see the report come up."

Noah laid a hand on his shoulder. "That's good, but I have no plans on letting you go anywhere."

Neil grinned up at him. "I was kind of hoping you'd say that," he said. "Trust me, if you let anything happen to me I can guarantee I will haunt you for the rest of your life!"

"Nothing is going to happen to you, Neil," Moose said. "You're our baby brother, anybody who wanted to hurt you would have to go through all of us, first."

"Got that right," Sarah said. "We gotta take care of the kid, right, Noah?"

"Of course," Noah said. "I know we're all supposed to be expendable, but this team isn't ever going to leave anyone behind. We stick together and do our jobs, because we're the best."

All three of the others looked at him for a moment, but then Sarah grinned. "I'm all for that," she said. "Nobody gets left behind, and nobody gets killed."

NINETEEN

"Everything's set for tomorrow, Boss," Neil said. "I've checked and double checked and triple checked, and even double checked my triple checking. If he actually makes that call, we're going to know where he's making it from."

It was almost ten o'clock and Noah had just announced that they needed to get plenty of rest. While the action would be handled by Delta Force, there would undoubtedly be a lot of after-action issues for the team to handle, and he wanted them to be at their best. Moose grabbed hold of Neil and dragged him out the door, while Sarah announced that she was going to the shower. Noah waited for a moment to see if she would invite him in, but then he decided it didn't matter and followed her through the door.

Noah awoke five minutes before his alarm was set to go off at six and rolled out of bed as quietly as he could. There was no point in waking Sarah so early, so he sat in one of the chairs and used his phone to check for emails or messages.

There was one email, and Noah's eyebrows went up when he saw that it was from Allison.

Camelot, it said, *I wanted to let you know that I'm still in possession of all my mental faculties and will be returning to my office sometime in the next week or ten days. Dr. Parker has been keeping me updated on what's going on, and I completely support his decision to let you go after Andropov. I realize that you aren't one who needs encouragement or back patting, but I think it's important to let you know that I have the utmost confidence in you to get this job done.*

Incidentally, I spoke with the President yesterday (can you believe the son of a bitch actually flew out here and visited me in the hospital? Wonder how they kept that out of the press!) and he let me know that he also supports what you're doing. As a first-year operative, you were originally designated a Q4, which means that you are expected to remain within mission parameters at all times according to specific orders, but you have shown such initiative and aptitude that he has authorized moving you all the way to Q2. That rating means that you are authorized to go off mission on your own discretion, the American equivalent of James Bond and his "license to kill." Any action you take will be considered to have been sanctioned by me, or by the government of the United States.

All that said, I want you to know that I expected you would rise quickly, but you've outshined even my most imaginative speculations. Good job, Camelot.

"What are you doing?" Sarah asked sleepily. She was peeking at him under half-lidded eyes as she lay there on her belly.

Noah looked up at her. "Got an email from Allison," he said. "She expects to be back at work next week sometime."

Sarah's eyes opened wider and she smiled. "That's awesome," she said. "You know, if anyone had ever told me that someone as nice as she is could do the kind of job she does, I would've said they were crazy. I mean, I know she has to make decisions on who lives and who dies, and I'm glad she's strong enough to do it, but in spite of all that she's a genuinely nice person. I really, really like her."

"She's definitely strong," Noah said. "I think she must have some incredible control over her emotions. Not like me, I know that she actually has emotions because I've seen them. She just seems to have the ability to turn off parts of them when necessary."

Sarah rolled over onto her back and rubbed her eyes. "Are the boys up yet?"

"I haven't heard anything from them. I woke up before the alarm so I thought I'd let you get an extra few minutes of sleep."

She yawned and then threw off the covers. "That's sweet of you, but I need to get up. Our late lunch yesterday meant we didn't get dinner, and I'm ready to go have some breakfast. Call Doofus and Goofus and get them up. Nothing's supposed to happen until eleven, and this place has waffles downstairs. I want waffles, give me waffles." She stood up and headed for the bathroom.

Noah punched the speed dial button for Moose and wasn't surprised when it was answered almost instantly. "Sarah wants waffles," he said.

"Waffles will work. We're both up. Meet you guys down in the breakfast room?"

"Sure, we'll see you there," Noah said. He ended the call as Sarah came out of the bathroom and began pulling on her clothes. "The guys are up. I told them we'd meet them down in the breakfast room."

She looked at him with a grin on her face. "Then you better get some clothes on."

They walked into the breakfast room ten minutes later to find Neil standing by the waffle maker. Moose was already at a table, eating a waffle that seemed to be swimming in syrup.

"Good grief," Sarah said to him, "how are you not diabetic?"

"It's because I burn the calories up so fast," Moose answered. "My body never has time to realize I've eaten anything."

Neil's waffle was done a moment later and Sarah took over the machine. She made one for Noah and set it in front of him before starting one for herself, but the machine was quick and the waffles came out hot. Noah waited for hers to be done before he began eating, and both Moose and Neil went back for seconds as soon as they could.

They talked about inconsequential things as they ate, killing the hour they spent there the best they could. Other hotel guests were all around them, so they couldn't discuss the mission or the upcoming likely action. Moose told them a risqué story about his days in the Navy that made Neil snort waffle through his nose as he tried not to laugh with his mouth full, and Sarah simply covered her eyes and refused to look at him for the rest of the time they were there.

They finished up at a little after seven thirty and went back up to Noah's room. Neil brought his computer and set it up, then checked to be sure Nicolaich hadn't called his daughter yet. He had not; there had been a few calls to her number in the past few hours, but they all came from within Moscow.

"So, now we just wait," Neil said. "Too bad we don't have a deck of cards, we could…"

Noah's phone rang suddenly, and he glanced at it to see Captain Hayes's number on the caller ID.

"This is Camelot," he said.

"Sir, this is Captain Hayes. I'm reporting all units on station. We're ready to go whenever you give us the word."

"Very good, Captain," Noah said. "I'll send the location to the number you gave me as soon as we have it."

"Yes, Sir, we'll be waiting." The line went dead.

"Delta Force guys are all in position," Noah said to the team. "Like Neil said, now we just wait."

"It's frustrating that we have to sit back and do nothing while the commandos take Nicolaich out," Moose said. "He should be ours, don't you think?"

Noah shrugged. "As long as they get him, I'm not gonna worry about missing my own chance to take a shot at him. Last time you and I tried to take him out alone, he got away. If only one of these teams gets to him, he'll be up against five of the deadliest fighters in the world. From what I've read and heard about Delta Force, any one of them is a match for a whole squad of regular soldiers. We'll do our job and let them do theirs."

Sarah, sitting on the bed, looked from Noah to Moose and back again. "This is one time I agree with the big guy," she said. "I was hoping we'd get to him ourselves. Even after yesterday, I'd still like to watch you put a bullet through his head."

"I'll even go along with that," Neil added. "I got a little shook up yesterday, I know that, but I don't think seeing Nicolaich die would bother me a bit. Matter of fact, I think it would probably make me feel a whole lot better about what we do."

"This is exactly why Allison recruited me," Noah said. "You guys are all thinking emotionally. Nicolaich hurt you so you want to hurt him." He shook his head. "That isn't the way to do these things. An elimination has to be done surgically, precisely. Assassination is a powerful tool, but it depends heavily on the element of surprise. Nicolaich Andropov is fully aware that we're coming for him and he's set a trap, so there's no element of surprise. In this case, Captain Hayes and his men are the scalpel that will remove this cancerous growth we call Nicolaich from the world."

The other three sat quietly for a moment, and then Moose mumbled, "Still sucks. I was hoping to get a couple of bullets into that son of a bitch myself."

Sarah leaned back against the wall and picked up the TV remote from the nightstand beside her. She pushed the button to turn on the television and began flipping through the channels, looking for something to watch and kill the time. HBO was showing one of the recent Tom Cruise spy movies and Neil asked her to leave it on, so she did.

Noah moved up on the bed beside Sarah while Moose and Neil dragged their chairs to where they could see the TV better. The movie helped to pass the time, and was followed by a romantic comedy. By the time the second one was over, it was almost a quarter to eleven.

"Let's shut off the TV," Noah said. "With any luck, Bridger was telling the truth and we'll have a location to give Captain Hayes and his men within the next half hour or so."

They moved to the table where Neil's computer was open and running, and Neil slipped on the headphones that were plugged into it. Twenty silent minutes later, the program on the screen came to life. A call was coming in to Marina Andropov's phone and the computer was showing frantic activity as it traced the call back to its source.

"It's an international call," Neil said excitedly. "A woman, presumably Marina, answered the call and it sounds like Andropov's voice, but he's speaking in Russian. Routing through Switzerland—Germany—New York, it's bouncing through New York—got it, got it, got it, it's a cell phone, GPS coordinates 32.877586 dash 100.12524! Getting an address, give me a minute —here it is, the address is 2674 North Harrison Street in Arlington!"

Noah quickly punched the address into the SMS app on his phone and sent it to all of the Delta Force teams at once. Seconds later, two messages came through the radio that he had placed on the table.

"Group 8 closest, en route. ETA three minutes."

"Group 11, backup, ETA four point five."

"That's two teams scrambling to get there right now," Noah said. "Is he still on the phone?"

Neil was nodding frantically. "Yes, yes, he's just yakking away! This guy acts like he doesn't have a care in the world, how crazy is that?" His fingers were flying over the keyboard. The monitor on the computer had been split into two screens, one of them still on the phone-monitoring program while the other seemed to be jumping around. "I'm trying to find a traffic camera or something in that area, see if we can maybe watch what happens."

"Unplug your headphones, and maybe we can hear it," Moose said. "I'd love to hear that bastard scream in panic, hear the shot that takes him out."

Neil snatched off the headphones and unplugged them, and

they could all hear the conversation, even if they couldn't understand it. The four of them sat quietly, their attentions focused on the sounds coming through the computer speakers.

Three minutes passed, and then five. The telephone conversation continued and seemed peaceful, almost jovial. The woman's voice was replaced by that of a child who seemed delighted to be speaking to the caller.

Suddenly the radio crackled to life. "Group 8 is on site, no target, I say again, no target."

"Group 8, recon," came Captain Hayes's voice. "Group 11, report."

"Group 11 is on site, confirm no target, I say again, confirm no target."

Noah looked at Neil, his face was ashen. "Boss, that's the coordinates! He's got to be there!"

"Group 8, sit rep," Hayes said through the radio.

"Nobody here but some teenagers, Sir," came the reply. "My tech is scanning for cell signals on site, wait one."

"Neil, could he be bouncing the signal through some kind of repeater at that location?" Noah asked.

Neil stared at his computer monitor, his head shaking from side to side. "I guess—yeah, he could. I got the number of the cell phone the call seems to be coming from, let me try tracing it." His fingers began flying over the keyboard again, and the monitor display began to change. "I can't—holy crap, that's what he did! Somewhere at that location is a…"

"Sir," came the Group 8 voice through the radio, "we found a cell phone wired to some kind of computer. It was hidden under a bush just outside the house."

Neil was nodding. "Yeah, that's what I was going to say, he made some kind of a relay setup. Back-tracing from that phone now—nothing, whatever that box is they found is the actual receiver, and it's pushing the call through that cell phone. I don't have a number on that box, I can't trace it."

Noah cell phone rang and he answered it instantly. "Camelot," he said.

"This is Hayes, are you monitoring?"

"Yes," Noah said. "My intel guy says that box they found is some kind of cell phone relay system. He could call into it from anywhere in the world, and it would use the phone connected to it to bounce the call for him. Tell your men to stand down, and we'll try to figure out what to do next."

"Yes, Sir," Hayes said, and the phone went dead. A moment later his voice came through the radio, telling his men to report back to the JSOC facility and await further orders.

"I just can't..." Neil began, but Moose cut him off.

"Let it go, Neil, it wasn't your fault. We know this bastard is smart, we just didn't anticipate this kind of thing."

Neil spun to face him and they saw tears streaming down his cheeks. "But I should have! I should've seen it coming! I just wanted this to be over, I just wanted to get the son of a bitch, and I didn't think it through as far as I should have."

"We're not done yet," Noah said. "All this means is that he fed Bridger that line about the phone call. There was some reason he wanted us to think we found him, and I'm not going to buy the idea that he was just showing off."

Sarah's eyes suddenly went wide. "Molly! He wanted us out of the way for something, he must be going after Molly!"

Noah picked up his phone and called Molly's cell number. It rang three times, but then she answered.

"Is your security tight?" he asked. "Nicolaich is in the wind, we thought we had him but he got away. He was trying to keep us distracted for some reason."

"I've got your people here, plus all the security in the building. You think he's ready to make his move on me?"

"He could be, I really don't know. Just tell everyone to go on high alert."

"I will right now," Molly said. "If I make it through the day, let's talk this evening."

"Deal," Noah said, and then cut the call. He turned to Neil. "If you had that box, could you figure out where the call actually came from?"

Neil nodded, his face still twisted in rage and shame. "Maybe. I could hack it and find out what frequency it was receiving on, or whether it was using a cell number of its own. There's a chance I might be able to—"

The explosion blew the door off its hinges and threw it across the room, and the concussion wave that followed knocked all four of them out of their chairs and onto the floor. They were dazed, groaning from the shock, but Noah was already trying to raise his head to see what was happening. His vision was blurred and his ears were ringing, but he managed to make out several men rushing into the room.

They were all dressed in black, and all were carrying submachine guns. Noah tried to reach for his pistol but his arms and legs simply weren't responding to the commands his brain was sending. He lay there and watched as Sarah was grabbed from the floor and dragged away.

Moose grunted but Noah couldn't make out what he was trying to say. He managed to turn his head to look at his backup man, but then two of the strangers stepped in between them, and another was suddenly standing just in front of him. He tried to look up, tried to see who it was, but then a heavy boot smashed into the side of his head and the world went dark.

TWENTY

Noah awoke to find paramedics bending over him. For a second he was confused, but then he remembered the explosion. He turned his head to try to look around, but pain in his neck made him stop and lay still.

"Just hold still, Sir," one of the medics said to him. "You've been hurt pretty bad, but you're gonna be okay. We're just getting your vitals, then we're going to take you to the hospital."

Noah nodded just enough to show that he understood. His ears were still ringing, but at least he could hear. He opened his mouth to try to speak but his ears popped suddenly and pain shot through his head. He grimaced, but then closed his mouth and tried to swallow. Even that hurt.

He was lying on a gurney, he realized. The lack of pressure on his lower spine told him that his Glock was gone, holster and all. He lifted a hand and tapped the medic on the shoulder to get his attention, then opened his mouth again. In a hoarse whisper, he said, "Where are my friends?"

The paramedic shook his head. "Don't know what to tell you," he said. "Cops called us out here and said there was one person with injuries. You were the only one here when we arrived."

Noah allowed himself to lie back again. "Cops?" he managed to ask.

Nodding, the paramedic said, "Oh, yeah, a bunch of them. Whatever kind of bomb it was, it blew off your door and the one across the hall. The cops really want to talk to you but we told them they have to wait 'til you get to the hospital. All we're trying to do is make sure you're stable enough to transport, you know?"

Noah nodded slightly again, then tried to relax. The medic strapped him onto the stretcher and then he and his partner lifted it up until the wheels locked into place. A moment later, Noah could feel every bump and jolt as they rolled the stretcher across various kinds of debris.

He was taken to an elevator for the ride down, and then wheeled out and placed in the back of an ambulance. Noah saw several squad cars, and a police officer climbed into the ambulance with him and one of the paramedics, while the other paramedic went around front to drive. No one spoke, so Noah stayed quiet.

The ride seemed to last about fifteen minutes, and then he was being wheeled into an emergency room. He was pushed into a room with several curtained-off sections and placed into one of them, the curtain pulled around its curving track to give him some privacy. The police officer started to enter, but a nurse suddenly grabbed his arm and pulled him backward.

The nurse came in a moment later and began looking him over. "Hi, there," she said. "You want to tell me what happened to you?"

Noah opened his mouth once, but nothing came out. He closed it and then tried again. "Bomb went off," he said. "Just outside my hotel room."

"Yeah, that's what I heard. Any idea how that happened?"

"Somebody wants me dead," Noah said in his gruff whisper. "I don't know why he didn't finish the job."

"Okay, well, let's get you out of those clothes. The EMTs think you might have a few broken bones in there somewhere, so we're taking you down to x-ray."

She helped Noah sit up and he cooperated as she helped him out of his shirt and slacks. When he was down to his underwear, she handed him the hospital johnny and helped him slip his arms into it, then tied it behind his back.

"Okay, lay back down. One of the orderlies will be here in a few minutes to take you to x-ray." She turned around and slipped out of the curtained area, and Noah could hear the police officer asking if he and another officer could step inside. She stuck her head back in and asked, "Do you feel up to speaking to some policemen?"

Noah nodded slightly, then just said, "Yes, please send them in."

She held the curtain opened as two men entered. One was a uniform officer, but the other was in plainclothes.

"Thanks for agreeing to speak to us," said the one in the suit. "I'm Detective Gravois and this is Sergeant Gallagher. We're kind of curious about what happened back at the hotel. Think you can fill us in?"

"I can give you some basics," Noah said, "but first, do you have my wallet?"

Gravois nodded his head. "Yes," he said. "Wyatt Wilson, right?"

Noah tried to grin. "Yes and no," he said. "Do you have access to a magnetic strip reader? Check out the one on the back of my driver's license and you'll understand a lot more. I'm a federal agent, working undercover. Do you happen to know anything about the people who were in the room with me?"

"Were there people with you when the bomb went off? We found signs of other people, but no one else was there when we arrived."

"Yes, there were three others. Two men and a woman."

Gravois turned to the Sergeant. "The lieutenant has Mr. Wilson's wallet. Give him a call and have him check that strip, would you?"

"You got it," Sergeant Gallagher said, and then he turned and went through the curtain again.

Gravois turned back to Noah. "Undercover fed would make sense, considering the firepower we found in your room. You're asking about others, so I'm guessing you were part of a team?"

"Yes, made up of myself and the other three I mentioned. Two of them were staying in room two oh eight, next door to mine. I'd appreciate it if you could have their things gathered up, but don't let anybody tinker with the big suitcase. It's highly classified equipment."

"I'll see what I can do. Meanwhile, what can you tell me about what happened?"

"My agency sent me here to try to capture a known terrorist and arms dealer who has been seen in the area. It looks like I was getting close, because he apparently decided it was time to try to get rid of me."

Gravois chewed on the inside of his cheek for a moment. "Would he have taken those other people? And if he did, why would he leave you behind?"

"The answer to the first question would have to be yes, but I have no idea how to answer the second. I would have expected him to kill me while he had the chance. I vaguely remember seeing several men rush into the room shortly after the blast, and—I think I remember seeing the woman dragged away. I think I must've blacked out after that, that's all I can remember. I suppose it's possible they thought I was dead already."

The detective switched to the other cheek. "Maybe. I think it's likely the others were taken because this guy thinks he can use them for leverage against you, or against your agency, anyway. Any idea what he might try to get from your people in exchange for them?"

Noah considered being honest for a moment, telling Gravois that the only thing Nicolaich Andropov could conceivably want would be a broken Noah Wolf. Trying to explain it would be too difficult, though, he decided.

"I'm not sure," he said. "Somebody way above my pay grade would have to figure that out."

"You said some of your equipment was classified. I take it you can't give me a name on this terrorist?"

"I'm afraid not, Sir. This entire mission is highly classified."

An orderly walked in at that moment, and looked at the detective. "Excuse me, I'm supposed to take this patient to x-ray."

Gravois nodded and stepped back. "Don't let me stop you," he said. "Mr. Wilson, I'll be waiting when you get back here. Something tells me we're not quite finished yet."

The orderly grabbed hold of the end of the gurney and began pushing Noah through the curtain and down the hall. They got into an elevator and rode up to the second floor, then got out and followed another hall for about a hundred yards. Noah saw the sign that said "Radiology" as the orderly turned him and pushed him through the door below it.

The orderly helped Noah slide onto the x-ray platform, and the next fifteen minutes were spent taking various pictures of different parts of his body. He managed to lie on his right side when he was asked to, but turning onto it caused considerable pain in his hip. Noah didn't complain, just gritted his teeth and put the pain out of his mind.

When they were finished, Noah managed to get back onto the gurney by himself and the orderly retraced his route. True to his word, Gravois was sitting in a chair only a few feet from the curtain that the orderly pushed Noah behind. As soon as he was situated, Gravois returned with Sergeant Gallagher beside him.

"State Department says we're not to hold you," Gravois said. "I don't know how I'm supposed to close this file, but I suppose that's for somebody above my own pay grade to figure out." He handed Noah a business card. "That's got my cell number written on the back. I'll make sure all your things are secured and not tampered with. You call me when you get out of here and I'll meet with you to see that you get it all back."

"I appreciate it, Detective," Noah said.

"No problem," Gravois replied. "State didn't say anything about getting in touch with you or anything. Would you like me to put an officer here to watch over you? If your arms dealer figures out you survived, he might come back and try to finish the job after all."

"I suppose that's possible, but I have my doubts. Whatever he's up to, I don't think he's going to risk exposing himself just to get me. Listen, I had a Glock pistol…"

Gravois grinned and nodded. "Yep, it was bagged and tagged. I'll see that it comes back to you with all the rest. I don't think you have anywhere under that gown to hide a handgun, anyway."

Noah raised one eyebrow. "Very good point," he said. "I think…"

He was interrupted by the arrival of a doctor, a thin older man of Middle Eastern descent. Gravois shook Noah's hand and said goodbye, and then he and Sergeant Gallagher turned to make their departure.

"Detective," Noah said quickly, "do me a favor and stick around for a few minutes, would you?"

Gravois grinned and nodded, and then stepped through the curtain.

"Hello," the doctor said with hardly any accent at all. "I am Doctor Patel. I've been going over your x-rays with our x-ray technician, and he tells me that you have some minor fractures in two of your ribs and on the far right edge of your pelvis. None of them seem to be very serious, but they may cause you some discomfort. If you like, I can give you a prescription for the pain…"

Noah shook his head. "That won't be necessary. How soon can I leave?"

The doctor's eyebrows rose. "I was going to suggest that you might wish to stay overnight, just so that we can keep an eye on you. You suffered primary and secondary blast injury trauma. It is possible that you may have internal injuries that won't show up on x-ray."

"I actually don't feel that bad, Doctor," Noah said. "I'll

promise that if you let me go, I'll come back if I start to feel like anything's wrong. Would that be good enough?"

The doctor let out a sigh. "I suppose it will," he said. "If you wish to go, you may do so. Let me complete your release documents, and the nurse will bring them to you to sign. Do remember, however, you could have some serious internal injuries. Do not hesitate to return if you feel the need. Any sudden increase in pain, any sudden pains or sensations in your head, they should be warning signs. Do not ignore them."

The doctor walked out of the exam area and Gravois stuck his head back in. "Need a lift?"

"I will in a few minutes. Give me a minute to get my clothes on and sign whatever paperwork they got for me, and I'll be ready to go."

"No sweat. I'll be waiting out here, the chairs are more comfortable than standing around."

Noah winced as he sat up and then slid off the gurney. The nurse had laid his clothing on a stool nearby and he was just putting his pants on when she came in again.

"Well, heck," she said. "I must be losing my touch. Here we've got a good-looking guy who really ought to stay with us for a couple of days, and he can't wait to get away. Time for me to go back to the hairdresser and get rid of this gray." She held out a clipboard and pointed at a signature line. "Sign right there, Bud, or you're not going anyplace."

Noah signed where she indicated and handed it back. "Sorry

about taking off so soon," he said. "Got work to do. And you don't have enough gray in your hair to worry about, but I'm engaged."

The nurse grinned. "Is that the excuse you use with all the women who think you're hot? Doctor says to remind you to come back if you have any problems at all." She winked at him and was gone.

Noah managed to get his shirt on and then sat on the stool to put on his socks, which was when he noticed that he didn't have any shoes. He'd heard about explosions snatching people right out of their footwear, and decided there must be some truth to it. He opened the curtain and spotted Gravois sitting in the waiting area.

The detective got up and walked toward him. "You got a bit of a limp there," he said. "You sure you don't want to stick around here a while?"

"Quite sure," Noah said. "There's a nurse back there who seems to think of me as cougar bait. I need to get out there and find my people. Incidentally, any idea where my phone might've gone?"

"Everything that was in the room has been bagged and tagged, but after Gallagher talked to State, we had it all put away in a separate locker. We never made it to the second room, so anything that was in there is still waiting for you."

The detective's car was parked in a special slot near the door that was reserved for police, and he opened the front passenger door for Noah before going around to get behind the wheel. "I'll take you to our storage warehouse first, if you want, so you can change clothes and look for your phone."

Noah nodded. "That would be appreciated. I hope my shoes are there."

"They probably are—like I said, everything got bagged and tagged. The lieutenant still has your wallet, but he'll meet us there."

"Good, I'm gonna need it."

TWENTY-ONE

Detective Gravois drove directly to the police evidence repository, a large warehouse-like building divided into hundreds of storage lockers. A sergeant at the front desk of the building escorted them back to the locker where all of the gathered evidence from Noah's room had been hastily stashed away on orders from the State Department. He opened the space and then left Noah and the detective alone.

"I hope you don't embarrass too easily," Noah said. "That's my suitcase, and I'm going to change clothes real quick."

"Never been in a police locker room, have you? Go ahead, won't bother me."

Noah laid the suitcase on the floor and popped it open, then stripped down to his underwear again. Ten minutes later he was dressed in jeans and a blue polo shirt, with a pair of sneakers on his feet. He stuffed his scorched and torn clothing into a trash bag that was lying on the floor, then began looking through the rest of the items.

A box marked "Devices, Electronic" caught his eye and he pulled the top off. Neil's computer was inside, along with the radio receiver Captain Hayes had given him and both his and Neil's cell phones. He picked up his phone and pressed the power button, and nodded when it came to life. The screen on it was cracked but it was still functional. He quickly scrolled through the menu to find the speed down button for Doc Parker, but then decided to wait until he was alone before calling in.

The phone buzzed suddenly and he saw the icon for voicemails appear, followed instantly by another for text messages. He slipped the phone into his pocket and continued looking through boxes. He found his pistol in the second box, still in its holster, and slipped it onto the back of his belt.

That prompted him to look for his lightweight jacket, and he found it in a box marked "Closet" and slipped it on. He turned to face Gravois.

"Obviously, I don't have any way to take all the stuff with me at the moment. Can it stay here for a day or so?"

The detective nodded. "That won't be any problem. Even when we return evidence to civilians, we give them a couple of weeks to come and get it. It'll all be safe here for now."

"Thank you," Noah said. "Now, if we can track down the Lieutenant with my wallet…"

"That would be me," said a short, chubby man as he rounded the corner into the unit. "You're Wilson? I'm Lieutenant Steve Lasher." He held up a plastic Ziploc bag with Noah's wallet inside and waggled it. "I gather you wanted to get your hands on this?"

Noah shrugged. "Since it's got my ID and credit cards in it, I thought it might come in handy."

Lasher laughed and tossed the bag to Noah. "So, what kind of fed are you? I called the number that came up on the strip reader and found myself talking to some stuffed shirt at the State Department, then I got transferred to the NSA. No, wait, let me guess: you could tell me, but then you'd have to kill me, right?"

Noah put a grin on his face. "That could be a lot closer to the truth than you want to think about," he said. "No, actually I'm part of a new counter-terrorism task force. My team is supposed to track down particular individuals who turn up on our radar. This time, it looks like one of them tracked us down instead."

Lasher nodded. "Nobody told us to stay out of the investigations into your missing people, so I've got the word out. We managed to get photos of them from the hotel's security cameras and sent them out to every patrol officer. If one of them turns up, we'll know about it. We're checking every hospital, morgue, you name it."

Noah looked at him. "I appreciate it," he said. He was still looking through boxes and suddenly froze. Sarah's purse was in a box marked "Personals," and he flipped it open. He dug around for a moment and came up with the keys to the Chrysler, then looked up at Lasher. "There was a small Beretta automatic in this purse. Any idea where it ended up?"

Lasher pointed to the duffel bag that Moose used for carrying guns. "All the firearms except yours went into that bag," he said. "Should be there."

Noah knelt down and unzipped the bag. Almost all of the guns, including Moose's Glock and Sarah's Beretta, were present. Even the air rifle they had bought was in the bag. The only thing missing was Neil's little machine pistol. He picked up the Beretta and shoved it into his pocket.

"I'm going to leave most of this here at the moment," he said as he picked up his suitcase. "Detective, could I trouble you for a ride back to the hotel? I can get a cab, if you prefer."

Gravois started to speak but Lasher cut him off. "I'll drive you," he said. "I got a private message I'm supposed to give you, anyway, from somebody named Parker."

Noah shook Gravois' hand and followed Lasher out of the building to his car. He tossed his suitcase into the back seat and climbed into the front passenger side. "What's the message?" he asked.

"I got a call just a bit ago from a guy named Parker, sounded like an old fellow. He wants you to call somebody named Donnie Franco as soon as you can. I guess he talked to the doctors at the hospital and found out you got banged up good, because he said he don't want you going solo on whatever's going on. He says Donnie Franco will help you get things done. Kinda weird, he kept saying it like that, Donnie Franco, Donnie Franco."

Noah nodded. "I'll be calling Parker in a bit, and I know who Donnie Franco is. I appreciate the message, though."

Lasher glanced over at him. "Can I ask you something?"

"Sure, go ahead. I'll answer you if I can."

"These people that are missing," Lasher said. "On the hotel security cameras, you all look like you were pretty close. You think there's any chance you're going to find them alive?"

"At least one of them," Noah said. "One or two may be dead already, though I doubt it. There wouldn't be any point in taking them along if they planned to kill them right away, it would've been easier just to put them down right there in the room. The man who took them will be planning on trying to use them to draw me out into a trap. I've just got to figure out how to turn it into a trap for him, instead."

Lasher shook his head. "Can't say I envy you," he said, "but if there's anything we can do, just let us know." He reached into his shirt pocket and produced a card like the one Gravois had already given Noah.

* * * * *

Some kind of noise was there, just under the threshold of being annoying. It had been there for a while, he knew, slowly worming its way through his eardrum and demanding his return to consciousness. The realization that he could hear reminded him that he could see, and he struggled for a moment to open his eyes. His entire body was in pain, and even his eyelids protested at being forced to move.

His eyes were open but he still couldn't see. He tried to move, and suddenly realized that his hands were bound together behind his back and he seemed to be tied to a post or something. He struggled for a moment but it only intensified the pain he was already feeling, so he stopped after only a few seconds.

"Moose?" A faint voice managed to cut through the ringing sound that had been the annoying noise. The voice was soft, and he knew it was Sarah.

"Sarah, it's Neil," he said. "Any idea what's going on?"

"Nicolaich," she said quietly. "There was an explosion. It blew the door off the frame and knocked you cold, but I was still conscious. He walked right into the room with other men, and they dragged us out."

"Oh, geez," Neil said. "Oh, shit! What about Noah and Moose, are they here?"

"Moose is here, he's over there by you someplace. He had a lot of blood on his face, he might be hurt pretty bad. They didn't bring Noah with us. I think—I think they killed him."

Neil was trying to wrap his head around the things she was telling him, but the ringing was making it hard to concentrate. "But you didn't see them kill him?"

"No, but why would they leave him behind if he was still alive?"

"Because that crazy Russian son of a bitch likes to play his games. If he took us but left Noah, it's because he wants to play cat and mouse. Oh, shit! Moose? Moose, wake up, man! Come on, man, we need you!"

"I'm awake," Moose said very softly. "I'm playing possum. Sooner or later they're going to come in here and need to move us. I'm trying to look as weak as possible so I can try to catch them off guard when that happens."

"Do you know if Noah…"

"I don't know anything for sure, but I don't think they would've killed him. Like you said, Nicolaich wants to play his games. If Noah is alive, you can bet he'll be coming for us."

"Do you really think so?"

"Remember what he said, this team doesn't leave anybody behind. If he's alive, he's trying to find us right now. If he were dead, they would've killed us already anyway, so I'm pretty sure he's alive. We just need to do everything we can to be ready when he comes, because we might need to create some distractions here in the background."

"How bad are you hurt?" Sarah asked.

"I've been a lot worse. I'm not hurt bad enough to slow me down much, if I can just get my hands free. As far as I'm concerned, these maggots that are helping Nicolaich all need to die with him."

"I second that," Neil said. "So what do we do now?"

Moose grunted. "Sit still, be quiet and try to rest. When the time comes, we'll need all the energy we can muster. Do your best to save your strength for when we really need it."

* * * * *

Lasher parked outside the hotel and walked in with Noah. With his help, the hotel staff agreed to give Noah access to the room Moose and Neil had occupied. That task finished, Lasher shook Noah's hand and walked away.

Noah went up to the room and entered it. It took him half an hour to pack all of their clothes back into their bags and load them onto the luggage cart. The last item he loaded was the big 3-D printer, and then he closed the door behind him and pushed the cart to the elevator.

He stopped at the front desk to check out, and the clerk told him how sorry she was that his friends had gone missing. Noah thanked her and then wheeled the cart out to the parking lot where the Chrysler was waiting. He loaded everything into the trunk and then got behind the wheel.

He took out his phone as he pulled out of the parking lot and pushed the button to call Parker. The old man answered halfway through the first ring.

"Camelot?"

"Yes, Sir, it's me. The whole thing with a telephone call was a set up, and I think I've figured out what it was all about. Nicolaich knew that I have someone who's good at the high-tech stuff, and figured we'd be able to trace a call back to him if we knew who he was calling. He sacrificed three men to make me believe we had that chance, but what he was really doing was having someone else trace right back to Neil's computer. He had our location at the same time we thought we had his."

"I'm afraid we've come to the same conclusion," Parker said. "And now he has your entire team."

"Yes, Sir, but he's tried this one with me before. He's going to try to use them to bait me into a trap, but I'm going to flip it on him again. Incidentally, I got your message about calling Donnie Franco. I'm assuming you were trying to tell me to call Captain Hayes from Delta Force? Enlist his help?"

"The message meant for you to call him, yes, but I've already enlisted his help. He's supposed to get you out of there, get you back here to Neverland as soon as possible."

Noah was quiet for a matter of several seconds. "Sir, Team Camelot has a motto. We say that no one gets left behind. I need to go after them, Sir, even if only to make sure they're properly buried."

Parker sighed deeply. "Camelot, you're too valuable. In a situation like this, I have to conserve my most valuable assets. In this case, that's you. If you go after them, the most likely scenario is that you'll get yourself killed. We simply can't afford to lose you, not right now. Your team, unfortunately, is expendable; you are not."

Noah frowned. "I understand, Sir, but I respectfully request..."

"Camelot, your orders are to contact Captain Hayes and allow a team of his men to escort you to Denver International. Our people will pick you up there when you arrive."

"Yes, Sir," Noah said.

"I know you're supposed to be emotionless, but losing a team is going to be hard on anyone, even you. Let's get you back here and patched up, let somebody else go after Andropov."

"Yes, Sir."

"Very good. I'll see you for debriefing day after tomorrow." The line went dead as it always did when Doc Parker had said all he wanted to say.

TWENTY-TWO

Noah looked at the phone and found the number for Captain Hayes, but his thumb only hovered over it. He knew what would happen if he disobeyed the orders he had just been given, but just as he had done in the desert of Iraq, he considered whether those orders conflicted with what he knew was the right thing to do.

He also considered the conversations he had had lately with Sarah, and with Moose and Neil. He had acknowledged that his desire for Sarah's happiness and well-being was a form of love, and acknowledged her own feelings for him. As far as the two guys, he had come to think of them as necessary to his life, which was probably as close to forming a true friendship as he was capable of coming.

If he didn't play the game, there was no doubt Nicolaich would kill them within a matter of days. Noah was capable of accepting that fact, but the logical necessity of abandoning them seemed to sit heavy in the pit of his stomach. He couldn't put a name to the feeling, but Noah realized that he was feeling an emotion for the first time in many, many years.

There was a conflict going on inside him, he realized, a conflict that was caused by some change in his personal makeup. In the past, back in Afghanistan, he had been forced on three occasions to walk away from men who could not be saved. He had never anguished over it, had never considered disobeying the orders to do so.

This situation was no different, except for that lump in his guts. The thought of never seeing Sarah, Moose or Neil again made that lump seem to grow.

Orders, however, were orders. Noah pushed the lump away as he picked up the phone to call Captain Hayes. It didn't even occur to him to make a mental apology to the three he was about to abandon to their fates.

Before he could complete the call, his phone rang, and the caller ID said the number was restricted. Noah squinted at it for a second, and then answered.

"Hello?"

"Ah, the indomitable Noah Wolf," said Nicolaich Andropov. "Are you ready for the next round of the game?"

"Where are my people, Nicolaich?"

"They are being kept in luxurious accommodations at the moment. That will change, of course, if you fail to cooperate with me."

"Why should I do that? You're going to kill them anyway, we both know it. Why should I give you any satisfaction when saving my friends is a lost cause?"

"Oh, but the cause is not lost. I assure you, Mr. Wolf, you most certainly can recover your friends alive and quite well. All it takes is some minor cooperation, and the four of you can be together again. You can take them home and tend to their injuries."

"And what kind of cooperation are we talking about?"

"The kind you are most suited to. There is an individual that I need to have eliminated. If you complete that mission for me, I will return these three, shall we say, negotiating points to you. If you refuse, one of them will die each day for the next three days. The one to die will be chosen by the roll of the dice, so I can't even tell you which one will be first."

"You've got plenty of assassins," Noah said. "Why would you need me to do your dirty work?"

"Let us just say that the target is an extremely difficult one. I feel confident that a man of your particular mental abilities can accomplish the mission, but I cannot imagine anyone else who might do so."

"Then that's what this has all been about? The attack on Neverland, everything, all just a ruse to get me in a position where you could blackmail me into killing for you?"

"That would be one way of saying it. What? Did you think I was still seeking revenge over Vasily? Bah, Mr. Wolf, come now. We are men of politics, of espionage, of Machiavellian manipulations and machinations that most men could not even conceive. Vasily wanted to be a part of that world, and he knew the risks. I no longer hold any ill will toward you over his death. Instead, I hope to take advantage of your considerable skills. And forgive me, please, for resorting to such subterfuge, but I couldn't imagine that you might have been available for hire. This particular situation requires the best, and you are, in my opinion, the best."

Noah thought hard and quickly. "First things first," he said. "I won't even discuss your target or your mission until I know for certain that they're still alive. I want to see them, alive and with my own eyes. I'll come alone and unarmed. All I want is to see them and speak with them."

"I expected no less from you. We will meet this evening at eight. Go to the octagon at Windmill Hill Park on South Lee Street at that time and someone will be waiting for you. You will be searched, loaded into a vehicle from which you cannot see out and brought to my location, where you will see your friends for yourself. Afterward, we will discuss the terms of their release."

The line went dead and Noah began planning. He scrolled through the contacts for a second, but then considered that Nicolaich had his number and could possibly be tracing or even listening to every call he made.

A sign just ahead caught his eye and he turned the car into a parking lot. One of the stores advertised contract-free cell phone plans and Noah hurried inside. Fifteen minutes later he walked out with a cheap folding cell phone and got back into the car.

Nicolaich had obviously gotten his number from Sarah's phone, which also had most of the important numbers from Neverland in it. Noah couldn't risk calling in to Doc Parker, just on the chance that Nicolaich might have traces on all of those numbers, as well. Still, he needed to reach someone back at headquarters.

An idea struck him, and he dialed the number for the Sagebrush Saloon. It was past noon, so there was a possibility Elaine Jefferson might be working.

"Sagebrush," a hostess answered.

"Hey, I was wondering if Elaine is on duty yet?"

"Um, yeah, just a minute." The hostess dropped the receiver onto something and yelled across the room for Elaine. Noah waited for about a minute, and then she picked up the phone.

"Hello?"

"Elaine, this is Noah. I need…"

"Oh, God, has something happened to Moose?"

"I can't go into that. I need to speak to Doc Parker, but I can't call in on the regular number. I need you to get a message to him, but you can't call on the regular line, either. Somehow, I need you to get word to him to call me as soon as possible on this number, but to call from a number that is not associated with Neverland.

Tell him that I have reason to believe that all of our phones have been compromised." He gave her the number of his new burner phone. "Can you do that for me?"

"Yeah, yeah, I'll—just tell me, is Moose okay?"

"As far as I know, he's fine right now. That's the truth, I won't lie to you. I just have reasons why I can't call in on normal channels, so this is very important. I need Parker to call me as soon as possible."

"Okay, I'll call my dad at home right now. He'll know an unofficial number he can call on."

She hung up and Noah sat in the car, thinking of how he might turn the tables on Nicolaich once again. There was one slim chance that came to mind, and he leaned back against the headrest as he tried to predict where the plan might have weaknesses.

His new phone rang only a few minutes later and the caller ID displayed a number he didn't recognize. He answered quickly.

"Camelot," Doc Parker said, "I received your message and I understand that our phones may have been compromised. What is your situation?"

"Sir, I was contacted by the subject a few minutes ago on my mission phone. He stated that he will return my team unharmed on the condition that I carry out a task for him. I told him I wouldn't consider it without seeing them alive, and I have a plan that I believe will allow me to rescue them and deal with the subject. I'm requesting permission to put that plan into action."

Parker was quiet for almost a full minute. At last, he said,

"Camelot, this is an unsecured line. Because it could be easily monitored, I cannot act in any official capacity at this moment. You had already received instructions prior to this contact. Failure to follow those instructions could, under company policy, result in termination. If you choose to implement your plan, it is highly likely that you will face a review. Do I make myself clear?"

"Yes, Sir," Noah said.

"Very good." The line went dead.

Noah looked up Captain Hayes's number in the mission phone and dialed it into the burner. It rang four times before it was answered.

"Roadkill Café," came Hayes's voice. "Who's this?"

"It's Camelot, but this line is not secure. I have a situation that could benefit from your assistance."

Hayes hesitated for a couple of seconds. "Dude, I got a call from some old guy who wants you back home on the reservation pretty quick."

"I'm aware of that, and I've spoken with him. What I've got going on is pretty well off the reservation, but it's critical. Has anyone countermanded your original orders to render me assistance?"

Again there was a hesitation, but then Hayes spoke. "Those orders have not been specifically countermanded," he said. "What's the gig?"

"Completing my mission and getting my people back. Let's meet at the place where we first shook hands. Can you be there in an hour?"

"We're there now. See you as soon as you can get here."

Noah closed the little flip phone and shoved it into his shirt pocket, then put the car back in gear and headed toward the JSOC compound. The plan had weaknesses, that was true, but it was all he had.

The drive took forty-five minutes, but he saved time at the gate. Hayes was there waiting for him when he arrived, and the guards opened up without a question. Hayes slid into the passenger seat of the Chrysler and looked over at Noah.

"So what have we got going on?"

"Andropov set off a bomb in my hotel and stunned us all, then grabbed my whole team. He called me an hour ago and told me that he'll give them back, alive and unharmed, provided I perform a service for him. I don't know yet what that service is, but it's a safe bet it involves the assassination of someone powerful. I told him I wouldn't even consider it until I see my people face-to-face and know that they're alive, so we have a meeting set for eight o'clock tonight. I've come up with an idea on how I can get my people back and kill Andropov, but I need backup."

"I've only got a skeleton crew," Hayes said. "When I got the call to escort you back home, I sent most of my people back to Bragg. There are ten of us here, teams one and two from this morning's operation, and we'll continue to follow your orders until I'm told otherwise."

"That's all I can ask. Right now, though, I need someplace I can set up some equipment."

"Our TOC is in the same room where you briefed us yesterday. Let's head up there."

When Noah stepped out of the car and turned toward the trunk, Hayes saw that he was limping and offered to help carry in whatever Noah needed. Noah thanked him, and pulled Moose and Neil's bags out of the trunk so that Hayes could grab the big case with the printer.

"I need that inside, and set up on a table. Then we're going to hope I can figure out how to use it."

"Damn thing's heavy," Hayes said. "What is it?"

"That's a self-contained 3-D printer that makes high explosives, forming them into any shape and color. I need to make a few accessories for my little rendezvous tonight."

Hayes put the case on a table and Noah opened it up. The rest of the men gathered around as the printer extended itself upward and the control computer unfolded from the side.

"Here's what I've got in mind," Noah said. "I'm meeting someone at Windmill Hill Park at eight o'clock tonight. That person will take me to where my people are being held, so that I can see them. Andropov will be there as well, so that he can try to get me to commit to doing what he wants. Since I don't know where I'm going, there's no way for me to prepare anything on site in advance. That means that the only things I'm going to have available to me are things I can carry in on my person." Noah pulled the chair over to the table and sat down in it. "I need a Colt forty-five, the old army style. Any idea where I can get one in a hurry?"

"I've got one," Hayes said. He went to a pile of gear on the floor near the wall and returned with it a moment later. He handed it to Noah, who laid it on the table beside the printer.

"I'm going to make some things with this printer that I'll be able to carry in with me. My plan is to be able to place them around the area where my team is being held and use them to take out Andropov's men and create a diversion. Then, if we can figure out some way you can follow me, I'm hoping you guys will come charging in to the rescue."

Hayes frowned. "I could put a tracer on you, but these guys you're dealing with are also pros. If they caught the signal, they'd either take it away from you or kill you." He chewed his bottom lip for a moment, then turned and called one of his men. "Jimbo! What's the range on your camera drone?"

Jimbo, a short but lanky Asian man, screwed up his face and thought for a moment. "Around here, all this city around us, I'd say about four miles for signal distance, but it can stay in the air for over three hours."

"Could you follow a vehicle through the city with it at night?"

Jimbo grinned. "I can follow a firefly with it if you want me to. What's up?"

Hayes indicated Noah with his head. "Our friend here is going to meet someone in a while and be taken to an undisclosed location. We need a way to follow him so that we can show up to save the day."

"Easy as pie, man. Just get me on site a little early and I'll park my baby where I can keep an eye on you. This little puppy is dead silent, I could be ten feet over your head and you'd never know I was there."

Noah looked up at him. "What about speed? I'm assuming our destination will be somewhere within the area, but we may be doing interstate speeds."

"No sweat. She can do better than a hundred miles an hour, ain't no car going to get away from her. I can follow you until you get in a vehicle, and then keep that vehicle in sight until it stops. All we've got to do is cruise along behind her, not even close enough for anyone to see us."

Hayes looked at Noah and shrugged. "Jimbo got tapped for drone training a couple months ago. He's been dying to give it a try."

"Sounds like he just got the chance." Noah was scanning through the saved items in the 3-D printer's database of designs. He selected a pair of clip-on holsters, one that would fit the .45, and another the right size for Sarah's Beretta, which was still in his pocket, and told the printer to make them. They would be thick and heavy, but he didn't expect Andropov's men to take them from him once they relieved him of his guns. "Now, here's the other part. These things have a detonator inside them, and they're far more powerful than any explosive you've seen before. I can program them to go off at a certain time, but I have no way of knowing when would be the best time to use them. They can also be detonated by remote control and I'm going to give that to you. You have to be within a mile of them for it to work, so when you see that I've gotten where I'm going, you wait fifteen minutes and then set them off. I'll find a way to put them somewhere in the room or the area before then. Then, as soon as they go boom, I need you guys to come in as fast as you possibly can. I'll be unarmed when I go in, of course, but I'm hoping to be able to relieve one of Andropov's men of a weapon after the explosion."

Hayes nodded. "Fifteen minutes," he said. "Just be sure you get those off by then." He looked at Noah's wrist. "No watch? How are you going to know when to duck?"

"One of the weird little habits I picked up over the years," Noah said, "is that I'm always counting seconds in the back of my head. It gives me kind of a built-in alarm clock—I always wake up exactly when I want to, that sort of thing. In this case, I can sort of 'set' myself an internal timer for fifteen minutes. I'll do that a few seconds before I step inside, so I should be ready to hit the ground just before you push that red button."

TWENTY-THREE

Noah drove up to the park ten minutes early, and parked on the north side of Gibbon Street, the southern boundary of the park. He got out of the car and unlocked it, then began walking across the grass to get to the paved octagon with a single tree growing in the center of it. He reached it in about three minutes and stood on the pavement while he waited for a sign of his escort. He had left his Glock with Hayes, but the weight of the two guns and holsters on his belt was at least somewhat reassuring.

A couple of minutes passed and he began looking around to see if he could spot anyone. The only people in sight seemed to be teenagers, but then he saw two men approaching from the opposite end of the park. He watched them carefully and became certain that they were the ones he was looking for.

The two of them walked up to him and one of them asked, "Are you Mr. Wolf?"

"I am. Let's get on with this."

The man looked at one another and then motioned for him to follow them. They led him through the playground and across a concrete bridge over a stream, and stopped when they reached a large Mercedes cargo van. One of them opened the back door and motioned for Noah to get in, and the other one followed him inside. The doors closed and a light suddenly came on.

"I gotta pat you down," the man said. Noah grinned and opened his jacket to show a holstered Colt forty-five on his right side and a Beretta on his left. The man reached slowly to take both guns from him, then slipped them into the pockets of his own heavier jacket before frisking Noah the way a policeman might do.

The sides of the van were lined with seats and the man pointed at them. Noah didn't need any further invitation; he sat down and waited for the truck to begin moving. He didn't have to wait long before he felt the big van pull away from the curb and head down the street.

"So where are we going?" Noah asked.

The man grinned and shrugged. "I don't have any idea," he said. "The guy up front, he's the driver. He knows where we're going, but I don't."

Noah grunted and leaned back. He closed his eyes and tried to visualize the distance and turns.

Surprisingly, the ride only lasted about twenty minutes before the van came to a halt. A moment later, the back door was opened again and Noah saw three men with automatic rifles aimed at him. It was obvious they wanted him to follow, so he did so without asking any further questions.

The van had stopped in front of a run-down concrete building. There were only a couple of cars in its parking lot, and only one door was open. He followed his escorts through it and found himself in a dark hallway. There was barely enough light to see at all, and he found himself brushing the wall with his fingertips to be sure he was going straight.

A door opened ahead of him and light flooded the hall. Surrounded by his escort, Noah stepped into a room that had obviously once been used in manufacturing.

Nicolaich Andropov was sitting in a chair at a small table in the middle of the floor. He smiled when he saw Noah and pointed to the chair across from him.

"Mr. Wolf," he cried. "It is good to see you again. Come, I have vodka waiting for us."

"This isn't a social visit, Nicolaich," Noah said. "First I want to see my people and then we can talk about whatever it is you want."

Andropov laughed. "Oh, it is as I told you before. You Americans never cease to amaze me. Here you are, surrounded by my men with their weapons trained on you, and yet you presume to make demands. Come, I must insist. Join me for a drink while your friends are brought in."

Noah glared at him for a moment, then walked over and sat down. Andropov poured vodka into a glass and set it in front of him, then picked up his own. "Let us make a toast," he said. "To a future of cooperation between us."

Noah picked up his glass and held it close to Andropov's. "I've got a better one. To the day I get to put a bullet through your other eye." He clinked his glass against the other, then tossed it back and swallowed it down.

Andropov grinned and shrugged, but drank.

* * * * *

"Somebody's coming," Sarah whispered. "You had any luck?"

"Nope. Whoever tied us up knew exactly what he was doing. Just keep your cool, don't give them any excuse to rough you up. Neil, keep that sarcastic mind of yours under control."

"You don't have to worry about that," Neil said. "I hate to admit it, guys, but I'm pretty much scared shitless right at the moment."

A key rattled in a lock and the door was pushed slowly open. Light came into the room and they could see three men step inside.

"Nicolaich said to bring you all to him," one of them said. He and one of the others stood back with small machine guns pointed at them while the third man quickly cut them loose. Once their hands and feet were unbound, he helped them stand.

"Follow me," said the man who had freed them. The other two stood out of reach as Sarah, Moose and Neil followed him out the door. When they had gotten into the hallway, the two armed men fell in behind.

They made a couple of turns and suddenly found themselves in a large open bay. Sarah barely bit back a shriek of happiness when she saw Noah, but she couldn't resist glancing smugly at Moose and Neil. The look in her eyes told them that she was trying to say, "I told you he'd come for us!"

Noah looked them over quickly and decided that they had not been tortured or beaten since he had seen them last. He nodded to them once and turned back to Andropov. "Bring them closer, I want to talk to them."

Andropov grinned and motioned for the guards to bring them closer. When they were about eight feet away, he held up a hand for them to stop.

"You guys doing okay?" Noah asked.

"Well, the accommodations aren't as luxurious as I prefer," Moose said, "and I can't say much for the entertainment, but at least we're still kicking."

Noah nodded. "That's the important thing," he said. He leaned back in his chair and then winced. Sitting forward again, he reached down and took off the holsters and held them up for Andropov to see. "These are digging into my cracked ribs," he said as he dropped them on the table. He leaned back again and looked at Sarah. "You okay, Babe?"

"I'm better now that I've seen you," she said with a grin. "Any chance you've come to rescue a damsel in distress?"

He shrugged. "You might say we're in negotiations on that." he turned back to Andropov. "Okay, Asshole, who is it you want me to kill?"

"It's actually one of my competitors," Andropov said. "If I were younger and had both of my eyes, I could handle him myself. Unfortunately, that is not the case. This man is very well guarded and never allows himself to be exposed. It will not be an easy assignment, but I feel strongly that you can accomplish it."

"I'll need every bit of intel you can gather on him. I mean everything, from what he has for breakfast to how many sheets of toilet paper he tears off. Can you give me that kind of information?"

"It's being gathered as we speak. Can I assume from your questions that we have reached an agreement?"

Noah waggled a hand in the air. "That depends," he said. "I'll agree, provided you let the girl go with me today. Otherwise, I'm afraid we're at a stalemate, Nicolaich, because I don't trust you not to kill them as soon as I leave here."

Andropov nodded, his evil grin still plastered on his face. "I suspected that would be your demand," he said. "However, I'm not ready to give in on that point just yet. First, I want you to show me the plan you come up with to accomplish the mission. If the plan seems viable, then I will agree to your request. You will, of course, remain as my guests until then."

Noah leaned forward in his chair again. "Damn," he said. "Next time you blow up my room, tone down the explosives a bit, will you? You cracked a couple of my ribs and my freaking pelvis.

Makes it hard to sit for more than a few minutes." He slowly got to his feet, and stretched his back and rubbed his hip as he did so.

He looked over at Sarah. "Still in negotiations, Sweetheart," he said, and then he turned and looked at Andropov again. "Mind if I at least get a kiss from my fiancé?"

Andropov's eye went wide and his grin turned into a smile. "Fiancé? Well, then I can see why you are so insistent on taking her with you." He shrugged and flipped a hand in the air toward Sarah. "Be my guest, of course."

Noah turned and walked stiffly and slowly toward Sarah and the men, keeping his eyes focused on her own. He could see tears beginning to run down her cheeks as he approached her, and he spread his arms when he was still a couple of feet away.

Suddenly, he slapped a hand to his hip and let himself fall forward, grabbing Sarah and crashing into Moose and Neil on the way. The armed men jumped backward, and Noah could hear Andropov getting to his feet, his chair skittering backward.

Inside his head, he was counting seconds as he tried to make all three of them stay down on the floor. According to his mental clock, he had now been within the building for just over fifteen minutes, and he was wondering when Hayes…

The explosion was deafening! Hayes was right on time, and the blast and heat rolled just above them, throwing the half-dozen men in the room into the walls. Windows up high on the walls blew outward and large pieces of the tin roof came crashing down. As soon as the initial blast was over, though, Noah scrambled to his feet and went after one of the guns that had been blasted out of the hands of Andropov's men.

He wasn't surprised to see Moose leaping for one of the others. He snatched up the first one he reached and spun, looking for Andropov, but dust and debris made it almost impossible to see in that direction. He moved forward carefully, watching for any sign of movement, and suddenly he saw it.

Andropov had watched him fall onto the others, and realized instantly that Noah was trying to protect them, shield them with his own body. That had meant there would be a blast, and so he had dived for the floor himself. He'd been a few feet closer to the table when the explosive holsters had gone off, but he was getting to his feet as Noah approached him.

And then he heard it, even over the ringing in his ears, the shrill siren sound of a scream of rage. Andropov was up on his knees, facing Noah, and at first Noah thought the sound had come from him, but then Sarah flew past. She had also gotten hold of one of the machine pistols, but she wasn't aiming it at Andropov. She was swinging it by the barrel, like a baseball bat, and its short, stubby stock hit him precisely in his ruined left eye. He fell back and she followed, swinging again, catching him on the ear this time. He dropped back to the floor and Sarah fell to her knees beside him, raising the gun up over her head and bringing it down again with all the strength in her athletic little body.

A dozen times she must've struck him, until his face was nothing but a bloody mass. When all of her rage was spent, she fell back, and that was when Noah realized that she was no longer screaming, but was sobbing. He knelt down beside her and put a hand on her shoulder, and she spun and threw her arms around his neck. She was crying so hard that she made him lose his balance and fall down beside her.

A three-round burst erupted, and Noah jumped away from Sarah to see who had fired—and then lowered his gun once more when he saw that it was Neil. He had picked up one of the guns and followed Sarah, adding three bullets in the chest to the fatal wounds that Nicolaich Andropov had already suffered.

Suddenly there were other gunshots, and moments later Captain Hayes and two of his men came rushing into the room. Moose had already rounded up the surviving mercenaries, and Hayes's men brought in several more that were found throughout the old building.

Hayes spotted Noah sitting on the floor beside Sarah and walked over to him. "Hell," he said plaintively, "you could've saved a little fun for us."

"Sometimes," Noah said, "people just need to do things for themselves."

Hayes looked at the ruined face of Nicolaich Andropov and then glanced at Sarah, who was still clinging to Noah and crying her eyes out. He turned his eyes to Noah's own and nodded silently.

* * * * *

The cleanup took a couple of days. Under questioning, some of the mercenaries who had been working with Andropov gave up the address of the house he had been using as a base of operations, and the FBI found evidence linking them all to the raid on Neverland.

Noah called Molly to let her know that Andropov was dead, and at her insistence, Noah and the team stayed at her house while they cooperated with the FBI and NSA. The day after the final confrontation with Andropov, they went and recovered their things from the police evidence building, and then sat through hours of debriefing by a team of FBI agents. When it was over, they were told they were free to leave.

"Well, you don't have to be a stranger, now that I know you're alive," Molly said. "Besides, me and Sarah need to sit down and have a nice long talk about you. I can give her some pointers on how to survive being in love with a Vulcan." She rubbed her hand on Noah's arm. "That girl has been good for you, Noah. I know you well enough to know you're going to claim you were just carrying out the mission, but something's changed. You're still not normal, but you are definitely attached to that girl. I'm glad to see it finally happened."

"I made a promise," he said. "I promised my team that we would never leave anyone behind. I keep my promises."

"I know that," Molly answered. "Just don't try to be something you're not. That's guaranteed to cause heartache for somebody, whether it's her or you or somebody else. Just keep being yourself, Noah. That's the Noah we need."

They said their goodbyes and Molly hugged each of them

before they got into the car, but then it was time to drive away. Sarah had seemed perfectly normal since she stopped crying after killing Andropov, so she was back behind the wheel and chattering away like always.

Moose and Neil were in the back seat, and when they got onto the interstate, the two of them started playing a game that involved finding a sign that began with each letter of the alphabet. They were doing fine, until they got to X. Finally, Neil pointed to a sign for a hospital that listed x-ray as one of its services, and they bent the rules enough to let it pass.

Both of the guys spent a lot of time on the phone speaking to their respective girlfriends back at Neverland. From the sound of things, both of the relationships were getting kind of serious, and Neil even asked Noah if he had any objection to Lacey moving into the trailer with him.

He didn't.

They stopped the first night at a motel in Illinois, then made it home the following night. Doc Parker had told him to take it easy for a couple of days after they got back, and come in for debriefing the next Monday morning. It was so late when they got in that they all stayed at Noah's house for the night, but the next day it was back to being just Noah and Sarah.

They didn't talk about the mission, or about what had happened at the end. Noah knew enough about psychology to realize that Sarah had to process what she had done for herself before she'd be able to talk about it, so he didn't press. They spent the weekend relaxing, and even took the boat out on the lake for a while on Sunday.

Mondays always come, however, so they reported to the office at nine AM, right on schedule. Art Jackson was there in the conference room when they walked in, and he pointed at the inevitable coffee and doughnuts. Moose was already there, and Neil had come in just after Noah and Sarah, so the four of them were sitting there talking with Jackson when they heard the door open.

They turned, expecting to see Doc Parker, but Allison Peterson stood there. She was using a cane, and her hair was a lot shorter, but other than that she was the Dragon Lady they knew and respected.

"Well, hell," she said, with only a slight slur to her words. "Did you save me any doughnuts?"

GET A FEW FREE BEST-SELLERS, AND EXCLUSIVE NOAH WOLF CONTENT

Building a relationship with my readers is the very best thing about writing. I occasionally send newsletters with details on new releases, special offers and other bits of news relating to the John Milton series.

And if you sign up to the mailing list I'll send you all this free stuff:

A copy of the prequel to the Noah Wolf thrillers, The Way of the Wolf. Learn and walk through Noah's horrific childhood, shady upbringing, and what exactly happened to mold him into the cold blooded killer he is today.

A copy of the opening novel in my bestselling Sam Prichard series, The Grave Man. If you liked Noah Wolf, then you'll love Sam!

Just for fun, I'll also throw in the *second* novel in the Sam Prichard series as well, Death Sung Softly. That's a quarter of series absolutely yours and ready to read for free.

Finally, you'll be eligible to enter exclusive giveaways I have for only my readers. The odds of winning are great since only subscribers on my mailing list are eligible to enter. Prizes include Kindles, Amazon gift-cards, Bestselling paperback and ebooks, and much more!

You can get the three novels, eligibility to the giveaways, and exclusive Noah Wolf content, for free, by signing up at

www.davidarcherbooks.com/vip

Enjoy This Book? You Can Make A Difference

Reviews are the most powerful tools in my arsenal when it comes to getting attention for my books. Much as I'd like to, I don't have the financial muscle of a New York publisher. I can't take out full-page ads in the newspaper or put posters on the subway.

(At least not yet, anyways!)

But I do have something much more powerful and effective than that, and it's something that those publishers would kill to get their hands on:

A committed and loyal bunch of readers.

Honest reviews of my books help bring them to the attention of other readers.

If you've enjoyed this book, I would be very grateful if you could spend just two minutes leaving a review (it can be as short as you like) on the book's Amazon page, or whatever other retailer you purchased it from.

Thank you so much!

Want More?

Check out ALL of David Archer's books on his
website:
www.davidarcherbooks.com

You can connect with David on Facebook at
www.facebook.com/authordavidarcher

Made in the USA
Las Vegas, NV
01 May 2021

22327584R00173